Sealed
In Fire

Sealed In Fire

Dream Writer's Chronicles
Book 2

Kelly Dowswell

Kelly Dowswell Books

First Published by Kelly Dowswell Books

Ontario, Canada

@Kelly.Dowswell

Book cover design moorbooksdesign.com

Paperback ISBN: 978-1-7386699-4-3

Ebook ISBN: 978-1-7386699-5-0

In loving memory of my Dad

One

Sarith watched the vein in the middle of Luke's forehead pulse. After fifteen years of marriage, she knew that vein well. It was in the shape of a lightning bolt and shot down from his hairline to his eyebrows. Today, it looked like it was pointing right towards his crunched up and bushy brows. She watched as the one eyebrow hair—the one that was longer than the rest—bounced up and down, up and down.

She was so focused on it she had stopped listening to the words being hurled towards her. And when he finally said her name, she realized she had been asked a question and had no idea how to answer.

"I'm, what?" she asked, looking away from the vein and the eyebrow hair, and meeting his eyes. She was always amazed at how icy blue and cold his eyes were, even while the rest of his face was so red and angry.

"Don't you care about our situation? Don't you care that our financial state is in a terrible place? Were you even listening?"

"Yes, I know where we're at. I know what's going on," Sarith said, thinking back to the last appointment at the bank. It was a huge stretch for them to get the money to buy the jewelry business that Sarith worked at, but they had scrimped and saved and somehow they had managed to get enough together to make the bank happy to give them the loan. They just had to finish the final paperwork with her boss Miles, and then they would finally own the business.

Sarith had worked there for the last five years, hoping for the day she could finally own it. She knew it would make an enormous difference for their financial situation. But even that aside, it would change things with Luke. Maybe he would finally relax and be more like the man he was when they first got married.

The financial stress over the last few years had really changed his personality into something she didn't love. He was shorter with her and had more angry outbursts. At some point along the way, it felt like he had turned against her, which she hated.

They had always been on the same side, but money...

"You're doing it again! You're not even listening to me!" Luke said, throwing his hands up in the air.

"I am listening! I know the situation and I know things need to change, but I can't exactly be hounding him all day, every day about it. He will sell it to us when he's ready. We just have to wait."

"Do you actually know? Do you actually?"

"Of course I do! Do you really think I don't understand the severity of the situation? I've been to every meeting with the bank. I'm working in the business. I have been there every time."

"But never listening. You need me to do everything for you."

Sarith's eyes snapped back to him. He had no clue what she went through every day: the worry, the stress, the pressure. How could he think she didn't have a clue? Of course she did.

"You have got to be kidding me! You can't seriously believe that?"

Luke shook his head. He never did like when she challenged him. He couldn't handle it. Sometimes, she just…

Luke turned away from her and walked towards their liquor cabinet. Pulling out the decanter, he poured himself a stiff drink. Taking a deep swig, he set his drink down and flopped into his chair, refusing to meet her eyes.

Immediately, the TV hummed to life, and he was finished talking. She shook her head and walked toward the kitchen and caught her daughter hiding on the staircase.

Melissa looked like a deer caught in headlights and quickly disappeared up the stairs as quietly as she had arrived.

Two

The bell jingled as the first customers entered the store. It was a young couple, and Sarith instinctively knew they were there for an engagement ring. Smiling, she approached them, and when they confirmed they were newly engaged and needing a ring, she showed them to the display case over on the far side of the store where the best rings were. She pulled out tray after tray, each one more beautiful than the last, but she could tell quickly they were more interested in window shopping than buying.

Sarith felt her joy sink. She needed to get another sale soon. The previous day had been a disaster.

The couple grinned and told her they would be back later in the day, but she knew she wouldn't see them again.

"Ma'am, how much is this gorgeous ruby necklace?" a lady asked, an hour later. She was the first person to enter after the first couple.

Sarith walked over and carefully removed the necklace from the display case and put it on a black velvet holder.

"This is such a stunning piece, isn't it? Van Cleef & Arpels made it in the 1960s. It was made for Audrey Hepburn. We have a certificate of authenticity to go with it. It's twenty-four carat gold and has Grade AAA rubies, which is one of the highest quality out there.

"It's one of my favourite pieces," Sarith said, moving the piece closer to the customer and encouraging her to pick it up.

"It's so beautiful!" The lady said, holding it up high in two hands, one cradling the main stone under it. "I can only imagine the cost..." she said, her voice trailing off as she put it back down.

"You pay for quality. This piece not only is gorgeous, but it has history too. It's really worth the price," Sarith said, feeling the hope of another sale slowly fading away.

"Oh, I'm sure I could never afford it then," she said as she walked away.

"But Audrey Hepburn wore these. They are worth the money. I assure you."

The lady took one more look, claiming she'd be back, but Sarith knew she wouldn't be back either.

The rest of the day went about the same. Only a few people actually bought pieces, but it wasn't enough to reach her sales goal. Every day this week it was the same. Every day she fell short, and it didn't matter the amount of marketing she was doing, it was a struggle.

She could hear Luke's words echoing in her head again. They swirled around and around like a typhoon... Of course she knew the reality of their financial situation. Of course she knew the stress. But she also knew how hard it was getting the people in. She couldn't exactly force them to come in. And everyday she couldn't wait to get herself out the door.

How was she going to buy this business when she herself couldn't even stand being here day after day?

But Luke was pushing this. He needed the money. He needed the new car and the big home. He needed the brand names and the fancy clothes. She remembered the days when all they needed were each other.

Not anymore. Those old high school friends had come back into his life and she watched as Luke was trying to keep up. She knew if she left today without asking Miles about the business that Luke would have something to say about it. As much as she didn't want to bug him again, she had to find her moment and ask.

Three

"Closing time," Miles said as he glanced at his watch.

"I'll get the door," Sarith said, more than ready for another long, sale-less day to finally be behind her. She hated these days. They all seemed to mesh together now. Each day, she was counting down the minutes until she could spin the open sign around.

As she reached the door, a man opened it and took a step inside.

"I'm sorry sir," she said, "we're just closing up. Is it possible to come back tomorrow?"

"Oh, I know. I'm actually here to see Miles."

Miles smiled as he walked over and shook the man's hand. It was a solid shake, and Miles patted him on the other arm a couple of times.

"John, good to see you! Let me give you the tour," Miles said as they went over to the other side of the store. Immediately, he showed him the different cases, and eventually to the cash register and the safe underneath.

Sarith watched, unsure what to do. Should she lock the door? Finish closing? She couldn't go home, not without talking to him about buying the shop.

Miles eventually saw her standing there watching and excused himself and came over to her.

"You don't have to stay," he said, his eyes more focused on John than her.

"Is John a new employee?" she asked, noticing that Miles hadn't met her eyes since John had entered.

"Not exactly…"

His tone of voice made her pause. She looked at him again; she could see something in his eyes. He wasn't telling her something.

"What is it?" she asked bluntly. She needed to get home and she didn't have the patience or the time to deal with this.

"John is, uh, the, well, he's the new owner of the store. Listen, I know we had discussed you possibly buying, but I just had to make a change fast, and honestly, I don't think you're cut out for it. He's an old friend and made me an offer I couldn't refuse." Miles said, nodding as John motioned him over and he walked away.

Sarith stood for a moment watching them, not sure how to get her feet to move. She was devastated. And how would Luke react? They had talked about it. They had planned for this and now it was gone. What was she supposed to do now?

"You can head home anytime," Miles said to Sarith. "We'll lock up when we're done."

Sarith pasted on a smile and headed to the back. She grabbed her purse and stopped at the doorway of the office. At one time she could see herself here, paying the bills, making the calls, and doing the things she had to do, but now she'd never have the chance. She could tell by the way this John person carried himself he wasn't going to be going anywhere. This had been her one chance, and it was gone.

Sarith walked past them and out the front door. She didn't know what she would do, but she needed to figure that out in the next few days. Working for someone new didn't interest her at all.

* * *

Sarith sat on the edge of the bed that night and waited for Luke to finish in the bathroom. She hadn't had the nerve to tell him the business sold. She knew it would make him fly off the handle and the last thing she wanted to deal with was that, yet again.

He finally came out and closed the door behind him.

"You need to ask again tomorrow about when we can sign papers for the business. He must be just about ready at this point."

Sarith kicked off her slippers and slipped her feet under the soft sheets. Luke had insisted on the Egyptian cotton, but she knew they shouldn't have spent the money. They were soft, but that money… it always came back to money with them. Always.

"I'm serious Sarith. We need to get this finalized as soon as possible."

"Luke, I know. Stop reminding me."

Luke sighed and turned away from her.

Big surprise, Sarith thought as she opened her book. She looked at the words on the page, but didn't read a single one.

Maybe she could find a new job, or a new business, and make the switch before he even knew she had lost the jewelry store. She decided the next day she would start her job search. There had to be a better-paying job out there somewhere, and then losing the business wouldn't be as painful.

She had almost convinced herself in those moments before sleep took her, but just as the dreams took hold, she knew it would never work. She didn't want to start over.

How would she tell him now?

Four

The days seemed to blend after the news of the store selling. Sarith headed into work each day and went through the motions. And almost daily, John was there, learning how to work the books. After the initial shock of someone else buying the business, she wasn't sure if she could work for someone else, but Luke's constant reminder of their financial problems made it all too clear she had to do it. She had to make it work and see if she could at least make it as the manager of the store. She had gotten the impression lately that John didn't plan to be there all the time and was hoping to get someone else to run the business.

The first few days weren't bad. John seemed genuinely ready to tackle the work, but as the days went by, she could tell they would not get along. He was so much like Luke when it came to being money focused that becoming anything more than just a sales clerk was definitely out of the question.

As he learnt more about how the business worked, he slowly watched her every move. The moment a customer walked in, he found something to do near her so he could overhear what she said.

He was constantly watching, not only how she made her sales, but also telling her what to say to land each sale. Anything she did that was outside of what he wanted, resulted in more conservations. Miles had given her far more freedom, and this new way of being managed was suffocating. She needed to get out of this job but she didn't know where else to go.

"Sarith, I need to see you in the office once you lock up," Miles said, heading back there himself.

She could feel the dread rising in her, knowing it was going to be another talk about her poor sales. The more John tried to micromanage her, the more she felt herself pushing back and the lower her sales went.

Sarith slowly flipped the 'open' sign around to 'closed' and locked the deadbolt. She reached up and pulled the shade down.

She took a deep breath and let it go as she knocked on the office door.

"Come in," Miles said, staring at the stack of papers on his desk.

She walked into the office. It had always been small, but today it felt like the walls were closing in around her. He motioned for her to sit on the chair opposite him at the desk.

"Is everything okay?" she asked, trying to sound confident, but the words stumbled over themselves and she felt silly.

Miles finally looked up from his papers and leaned back in the chair. He took a deep breath and just as he opened his mouth to speak, Sarith interrupted him.

"I know what this is about, and I'm sorry. I've been trying to get my sales up, but it's just that time of year, you know how it is. There's always a slump because people know Christmas is coming and everyone is waiting for the Black Friday sales."

Miles held up his hand, and Sarith's words stopped short.

"It's not about the sales. I know this time of year is tough. This isn't about that. It's about something else," he said, pausing for a moment. "Actually, let's go out to the front. Grab your bag too." He got up leading the way toward the front of the store where the antique necklaces were on display.

"Did you get something new?" she asked, feeling like there was going to be more to this conversation.

"No. Do you see anything missing?" he asked as he stood behind it.

She didn't even have to look too hard; she instantly saw it. The ruby necklace wasn't on the stand like it had been the other day. It was her favourite piece. She had just shown it to a couple. Maybe they had come back and gotten it when she was off the other day.

"You sold the ruby necklace!" she said, a grin creeping across her face.

"No, it wasn't sold. It's missing."

"Missing? How?"

"You tell me," Miles said, his eyes piercing. "A receipt was made for it, but absolutely no money has shown up for it."

"How is that possible?"

"You tell me. You were the last one around it the other day."

"What are you trying to say?"

"Where is it, Sarith?" he asked, walking around the glass cabinet and crossing his arms.

"Are you accusing me of something?"

"Well, I finally told you I sold the business to someone other than you. Then suddenly, a piece of jewelry you love goes missing. There's some receipt for it, but absolutely nothing in the safe or the account for it."

"I can't believe you would even think I'd do something like that. And when was I supposed to have done this?"

"During the thunderstorm the other day when the power glitched. I think you might have messed with the videotapes."

"How would I possibly know how to do that? And do you really think I would do something like that to jeopardize my job?"

"I think you're about to leave this job. I think you're mad about the way things went down and I'm sorry you feel that way, but it is what it is. I know you wouldn't have been able to handle running a business like this. You would have run it into the ground, and I was not about to stand by and watch my life's work be destroyed. This business has been in the community for far too long to have it fall apart."

"But you think I have what it takes to steal something? You have no proof!"

"No, because your timing was perfect with the power being out. The cameras were off. I've filed a police report and I've made my suspicions clear."

Sarith heard footsteps. Behind her were two large men, both in dress shirts and pressed pants.

"What's going on?" she asked, eyeing them.

"They are going to make sure you leave, and with nothing extra in your pockets."

Miles nodded at them and they both motioned for Sarith to lead the way.

"You have no proof I did anything of the sort. You accusing me like this! It's—It's just ridiculous! Expect to hear from my lawyer!" Sarith screamed at him. She turned back to the men, pushed her way through, and stormed outside.

The door closed behind her.

Sarith felt the anger in her rising. How could he do this to her? She looked at the store one last time, flipped it off with both hands, and walked away.

Five

Sarith walked through the door of their home and slowly closed it behind her. Luke was in the kitchen, the cooking utensils clanging on pots and pans as he made dinner. The smell of garlic, onion, and butter wafted toward her. He had just started, but she knew it would be good. Luke was an artist in the kitchen. Anything he made was always so good. It was almost annoying how good he was at it.

"Hey, is that you?" he asked, poking his head around the corner.

Sarith flashed a quick smile. She had been dragging her feet about how to tell him about the business selling and now it was harder that she didn't even have a job. He had put everything into this venture and now it was gone. All of it.

"I'm going to change. I'll be right back," she said, tossing her bag in the hall closet.

"No prob!" he replied as he disappeared back into the kitchen.

Sarith took a deep breath and walked toward the staircase. That staircase had been one of the selling features of the house. She could still remember the first time they had walked in and saw it. The staircase curved up to the left to the bedrooms above. The handrail was a deep mahogany and shone brightly against the afternoon light that filtered in the front windows.

The previous home never had handrails, only cracked plaster walls with hand smudges where the railings should have been. But she didn't mind. She had the plan to fix it, but with the stress of trying to buy the business, she hadn't gotten there yet. If she had had the chance, she would have torn out those old plaster walls and replaced it with barn boards. The handrail would have been handmade and so smooth splinters didn't stand the chance.

But it was Luke who needed this house: the house with the extra bedrooms that were just filled with things he never used. It had the big garage he claimed he would use but never went in and the tools sat as new as the day they were bought.

She would have been happy in the small house they used to own. She just needed more time to do the repairs she wanted to do, and the money seemed to go as fast as it came in.

The bedroom door creaked close, and she put on a pair of jeans and a loose t-shirt. She glanced in the mirror quickly but avoided making eye contact with herself. She knew if she looked into those green eyes of hers that she would fall apart.

Heading downstairs, she stood for a moment in the kitchen doorway, watching Luke and Melissa as they sat at the kitchen island. Melissa threw her head back, laughing.

"Mom, come here! You have to hear this," Melissa said, as she caught her breath and pushed her long brown hair behind her ear. Sarith took a deep breath and went over to them.

Even at fourteen, Sarith could see her daughter was growing into a beautiful woman. She was always smiling and forever an optimist. She could put a happy spin on anything that happened. Maybe that would help this news go down a bit better.

Melissa was telling her something, but already she had lost track of what was being said. The time was now to tell them, but she didn't want to. How was she going to? Luke peered over at her, and she could see it in his eyes. He already knew something was wrong.

"Sorry, I have something to tell you both," she started.

Six

Sarith put the last few dishes in the dishwasher. They went in with a clink, but she didn't even hear it. Her ears were perked, listening as Melissa ran up the stairs. Telling her and Luke the news went just as well as she expected. Melissa had freaked out and ran upstairs. Luke's silence spoke volumes; she felt the chill radiating from him, like the spring thaw of an iceberg.

Luke turned toward the stairs, and when he heard Melissa's door slam shut, he came back to Sarith.

"Well," he said, leaning against the far cabinets, his words cutting the silence like a knife.

"Yeah…" she said, her voice trailing off.

"How could you get yourself fired? How? We needed that job. We needed the money. And you went off and did that?"

"I didn't do it on purpose," she said, spying a dried splash of spaghetti sauce on the cupboard beside her. She scratched at it with her thumb, the red substance now a thick goo that rose up her nail.

"Good grief Sarith. We were going to buy the business. We had everything lined up. Oh crap. Our credit. All the money we moved around. All the steps we had taken. Are you freaking serious?" he asked as he walked over to her.

"What do you expect me to say?" Sarith asked, flicking the goo into the kitchen sink behind her. She looked Luke dead in the eye. She knew that look. He was going to scream at any moment. And she knew she would have to tell him to be quiet yet again. Only today she didn't feel like it. Today she wanted to yell back because, just like him, she was mad the deal was off. She hadn't planned any of this, and she couldn't do anything to change what had happened.

"Something! Anything!" he yelled again.

"I'm just as upset about this as you are!" Sarith yelled back, leaning toward him.

"Yeah, right," he said, rolling his eyes.

"What? I'm not allowed to be as upset as you now?"

Just as he opened his mouth to reply, a bang happened near the door Luke had just been at. It was Melissa, leaning up against the doorway. She had knocked the cupboard shut that was open a hair.

"Do you guys seriously have to scream at each other again?" Melissa asked. Sarith knew Melissa had heard them before, but the boldness she spoke with showed her it was probably more often than either she or Luke wanted to admit.

Luke backed up and turned to Melissa.

"I get it. You guys are mad. You're always mad about something with each other. Honest question, did you guys ever get along, like back when you first met? Did you ever just talk to each other without screaming?"

How had they gotten this angry at each other again? When had they stopped having each other's backs?

Sarith remembered the first date like it was only yesterday. She had been working at a restaurant when Luke and his coworker came in. They were there for lunch, and the first moment she spotted him, she was smitten. He had dark hair, done just so, and was much taller than her. He was nearly six-foot-five. But it was his blue eyes that had mesmerized her. She had never seen eyes so bright and radiant before, and something about them had come across as so warm. And of course, she had made a fool of herself waiting on them. She had dropped his water on his lap, had totally forgotten to take his coworker's order, and then brought him a second drink even though he never ordered it.

Luke had paid the bill for both him and his coworker, and had written his phone number on the receipt for her. He wanted to leave it up to her to make the first move, joking that the next time the drinks would be on her.

It had taken Sarith a week to get up the courage to call him. She usually never made the first move. Ever. So she dialled the number, fingers shaking, and listened to it ring. She was just about to give up when finally on the fourth ring, he answered, sounding flushed like he had just run for the phone.

After that, they didn't stop calling each other. And only six months later, they were engaged, and a few months later, they married in a small chapel on a weekend get-away.

That was fifteen years ago, and although they had a lot of good years, the last few years weren't going as well. They had been fighting more and more, mostly about finances. And when the option of buying the jewelry business came up, it was finally a common ground that they halfway agreed upon. Luke had pushed it more than she had wanted, but maybe if they did this, they would finally start getting along better. Having it fall apart like this was the last thing either of them needed. Sarith had thought this business was going to help their relationship, but now she didn't know what was going to happen. She hoped things would work out, but after this fight, she wasn't so sure.

"Everything's fine," Luke said, walking over to Melissa and putting his arm around her.

She gave him a look and Sarith knew Melissa didn't believe him, but she said nothing.

"Listen, go grab your jacket and we'll head to the mall for that book you were talking about the other day," Luke said, giving her a light squeeze and sending her upstairs.

Sarith looked into the kitchen sink. The spaghetti goo was softening and starting to crawl its way down towards the drain. Amazing how one conversation could make her feel about as good as that softening goo.

Seven

The house had been quiet since the day Sarith told her family about her job. Luke tried to be calm, but she could tell he was mad. They both had thought it was going to be the start of something so much bigger for them. Sarith had taken some business classes earlier in the year, so when she took over the store, she would be ready. They had extended their credit so she could do it, and now, it was all for naught. They didn't have the money for her to build her own business from the ground up, so the only other option was to buy one, and unless something major happened, she couldn't see anyone walking away from their livelihoods. And with the economy going the way it was, she would need something fast. Being an expert jeweller didn't have a huge market.

The day she called her mother about all of it, she expected the worst. Her mother's disappointment in her over the last few years had only grown. When she had told her mom she wanted to buy the business, it was the first time in years her mother hadn't openly criticized her choices.

Now it was gone though, she could only imagine what she would say.

"I have something to tell you," she started as her mother answered the phone.

"Yes?" came the curt reply.

"I, um, I…"

"What is it?"

"I'm not buying the business after all."

The silence on the line echoed loudly in her ears.

"I'm not sure what I'm going to do now," Sarith said, hoping her mother would at least say something.

"Do you have any other prospects?"

"Not at the moment. I don't really know what I'm going to do."

Her mother took a deep breath and let it out slowly. When she was done, she finally said, "Good."

"Good?" Sarith asked, wondering if she was hearing her wrong.

"Yes, it's about time you get out of these silly professions and start doing what I know you have wanted to do since you were young."

"What are you talking about?"

"Renovations. Building. Construction. You were in construction class in high school for four years. You built a deck at a neighbour's house, you made a gorgeous cedar chest that you still have today—who knows where—in your basement. Why do you keep avoiding it?"

"It's just a hobby…"

"You have made built-ins all over your house, you've made so many tables and chairs, and you have decked out your garage to the nines. And speaking of decked out, you built both a front and back deck on your house and a gazebo. What about the shed in your backyard? You started building it and if memory serves, it's still in pieces."

"I got busy…" she said, letting her voice trail off.

"Listen, you need to stop following all these other silly and fleeting aspirations and finally pursue the dream I know will make you actually happy, and that's the line of construction."

Sarith didn't want to admit it, but her mother was right. It was always something she had loved, even when she didn't expect to. She had taken the extra credit to boost her grades in school and it wasn't until she came home with her first wooden shelf—just a simple adjustable shelf—that she knew this was something she loved to do. The next year, the class was to make a bookcase. It was only supposed to be two feet tall, but Sarith had made hers five feet tall with adjustable shelves and spindles as an accent.

After that, the teacher let her make whatever project she wanted as long as she followed the few new techniques he taught at the beginning of the year. But she never went the simple route. She would add spindles she made herself or she used joints the teacher hadn't even mentioned yet, or have something done faster than the rest of the class.

Her talents didn't go unnoticed, however. The table she sat at had mostly good guys, but there was one that always had an opinion on everything. It started simple enough, pointing out the first couple of mistakes she made, then as she got better, it shifted to insults about how, as a girl, this wasn't the place for her. The comments got more pointed as the years went on about how she should be out of the construction site and in the home. Nothing Sarith said or did would make this guy stop. And on the last day of classes when Sarith was picking up the cedar chest she had made, she found it had been spray painted to say *Stay Home*. It wasn't enough to be pointedly sexist like his comments in class, but now he was vandalizing her work. She reported it, but without proof, there was nothing they could do and the student went off free, especially since it was the last day of classes and she knew she wouldn't see him again.

But that vandalism was more than paint on a piece of wood to her. It took her months before she even felt like sanding it out. Then when she did, it took hours to get it all down to a smooth even surface that she had to stain again and clear coat.

That one act had ruined construction and woodworking for her. She couldn't stand the sight of a sander anymore. Part of her wanted to get rid of the cedar chest, but Luke had convinced her to keep it. He liked it and didn't want to see her work tossed out.

So, she kept it in the basement. It was still there, covered up by a stack of blankets and towels.

"But what about that guy..." Sarith started, but instantly her mother cut her off.

"I don't care what the twerp from high school did or said. You are good at what you do and it shouldn't just be a hobby anymore. It needs to be something you do with your life. You are good and you need to forgive and let yourself do something I know you want to do."

The shift in her mom's opinion stopped her dead in her tracks. Her mom had always given her such a hard time since marrying Luke with the direction she chose for herself. When Sarith told her about the jewelry store, she pursed her lips and said if it would make her happy, then she guessed she was fine with it. Yet, now when she lost the job, her mom was oddly happier.

After Sarith got off the phone, she went to the basement and pulled the blankets and towels off the chest before opening it up. The smell of cedar was a comfort to her. It brought her back to the days of working with the tools and taking the care and time to create this piece. She had been so proud of it. Carefully, she hauled it upstairs to her bedroom and stared at it a long while. Sarith put it at the foot of the bed and sat on it, running her hand over the wood.

Maybe she should give it a shot again.

* * *

Sarith was waiting when Luke walked into the house. He clearly wasn't expecting her and was startled at seeing her.

"Sorry, I just wanted to talk to you about something."

"Just give me a sec," he said, tossing his briefcase down and heading towards the kitchen. He grabbed a glass, threw in some ice and filled it with bourbon until the ice floated. Taking a long drink, he set it down and pulled off his socks, which he flung into the corner of the kitchen. He knew she hated when he did that, but she could tell it wouldn't matter to him today. It must have been a bad day at the office if that's the first thing he did upon getting home.

Sarith leaned against the counter and waited until he motioned she had the floor.

"I spoke with my mother today," she started and immediately she saw his eyes roll. "I know, but this conversation was pretty good."

"Mmmm," he muttered as he took another large swig and walked over to the living room. He sat on the couch, putting his feet up on the coffee table. Another thing she couldn't stand.

"Remember how I told you I did construction classes back in high school?" she said, after following him to the other room. "Well, mother reminded me how much I loved these classes and I was actually pretty good at it. I was the one everyone wanted help from in the class. I did my own assignments because I just knew what I was doing. But after high school, I stopped. And I really think I should get back to it. I always loved it. The cedar chest even shows how good I am at it."

"It is pretty nice," Luke said, putting his glass down and sitting up now.

"Thanks. I was thinking maybe I could get a few tools and some wood and start making things to sell. I could post them online or at vendor shows or whatever."

"Well, but that would be a bit of an investment, though; having to get all the tools and the wood, and with prices the way they are," he said, his voice trailing off.

Sarith had been saying this to herself all day, but she had hoped he would not go down that road. They had a little they could use towards it now that they weren't buying the business and she really didn't know what else she would do with her time otherwise.

"We can look at things, but for now, maybe you should think about just getting a full-time job and we can wait and see how things go. We don't have much to sink into a new venture, especially if we don't know if it'll work out," Luke said, giving her a look that she knew meant the jewelry business.

Sarith nodded, knowing the conversation was already over. Luke got up and headed to the kitchen. She didn't follow him, but she heard the bottle of bourbon and the splash as he poured more. The bottle clanked when it hit the counter and he walked downstairs. She knew she wouldn't see him again for the night. Instead, he would lose himself in his bourbon haze, watching the old westerns she wasn't even sure he liked.

Eight

Weeks had passed since Sarith and Luke had talked about the woodworking business. She had tried to approach it again, but every time, Luke had had a bad day, so he went straight to the booze instead of wanting to talk to her, or he would head out with the buddies from before they were married. They were the very friends she couldn't stand and were giving him advice he was taking instead of listening to her. Every day that it happened, she could feel the distance growing between them and she felt like she was losing him.

Her phone rang in her pocket. Pulling it out, the name of the school was on the display. She sighed and answered. The principal again.

"What is it this time?" Sarith asked as she closed her car door.

"Well, this time she was part of a group that was picking on someone else. She didn't do any of the violence, but she was cheering them on, and we've seen her with them a lot lately. I'm concerned," said the principal who she'd known for years.

"I understand," Sarith said, buckling her seat belt. "But if she isn't actually doing anything wrong this time, then please, just let me handle the situation on my own. I have a lot going on and I am working on things as best as I can."

"I'm not trying to cause problems. It's just I know this crowd. And like I said the other day when we talked, she's starting to get herself into trouble. This group will absolutely lead her towards a suspension if she's not careful.

"I've seen a huge change in her. She's withdrawing from the group of friends that was good for her and she's getting more and more angry. The aggression will follow if we don't act soon."

"'We?'" Sarith said, feeling the anger tingling in her neck. "No. There's no we. There's me. I'm doing this. I will take care of things myself. For now, just back off and let me do what I need to do with my daughter."

She smashed her finger against the end call button and resisted the unhealthy urge to throw the phone.

This issue with Melissa, coupled with the fact that the job searching wasn't going well, was crushing her. It didn't seem to matter what she did. No one was interested in hiring her as a sales clerk. Part of her wondered if Miles was calling around and telling people not to hire her. She had even tried going to construction companies to see if she could get a job doing that, taking pictures of her work with her as proof she could do it, but with no apprentice-ship in that field, no one was interested.

She had just left another interview. The lady doing it had pity in her eyes and Sarith knew she wouldn't be hearing from her again. She drove through the city, unsure where to go next. She really didn't have anywhere she needed to be. It was another quiet day, with that being her only interview.

The roads were quieter today than she would have expected on a Monday morning, but she was thankful. If anyone had gotten in her way, she'd likely run them off the road.

Sarith finally stopped and found herself at a city park. She barely remembered the drive as her mind raced with thoughts she didn't want to think. What if they lost the house? What if her family blamed her? She hated thinking like this, but she couldn't make it stop.

And sometimes, it wasn't the yelling that got her the most scared. Sometimes, it was the silences in between: the long stares, the cold shoulders, the avoiding eye contact. Those were the hardest parts. Often she thought if they could just yell it out, it would make everything better. But then, maybe it wouldn't.

The boardwalk was empty this morning. Seagulls squawked in the distance as she peered over the water. Even the bay was quiet. Only a few anglers were out, and most were sitting with a cup of coffee in hand.

Her shoes clicked along the cement walkway, and she instantly regretted her choice of shoes. She should have grabbed her runners. But she wasn't thinking about that. She was thinking about everything else.

It was unusually warm for September, and she quickly took her jacket off. Ahead of her, someone was slowly biking along the waterfront, clearly enjoying the moment. They got off their bike and pulled a digital camera out of their bag and snapped a few photos.

As Sarith got closer, she recognized her. It was one of her longest friends, Meredith. They had met in first grade and had gone through school together. They grew close and when Sarith's parents had gotten into the fight at the homecoming football game, making all eyes turn to them, Meredith was the one that got the crowd's attention back to the game instead of their fight. Sarith had always been grateful for that.

"Sarith! It's been so long. How are you?" Meredith asked. Once high school was over, they went to separate colleges, but they always remained close, talking at least once a week and any time something big happened in their lives, they always showed up for each other.

"I'm doing alright," Sarith lied. "What are you up to?"

"Oh, I'm just on vacation this week, then it's back to snapping pictures," she laughed as she tilted the camera in her hand. "I have to get my own picture taking in some-times. But next week, I have a shoot in Iceland. Someone commissioned me to do it. My name is really getting out there."

"That's wonderful," Sarith said. A swell of embarrass-ment rose in her and nearly threatened to choke her. Her friend of years was doing what she loved, when Sarith herself felt like she was really doing nothing. And since losing her job and the chance to own the business, she felt even more like a failure. How would she explain herself now?

"I, uh, I heard about the store," Meredith said after an awkward moment between them.

"Well, not everything you heard was probably true," she said, crossing her arms and looking down at her feet.

"I didn't say I believe it all."

Sarith shifted her weight to her left leg and met her friend's eyes.

"Life is unfair," Meredith said. "I don't know everything that happened, but I am willing to believe there is more going on here than just what I've heard through the rumour mill, which I've been trying to put a stop to for a while now. But regardless of what happened, you just have to pull yourself back up by your bootstraps and move on. Hit the pavement as they say. Something will come up. Go for a hike. It'll clear your head and then you can go from there to figure out what to do next. That's always worked for us before."

"Yeah, I guess so," Sarith said, glancing at her watch, trying to make it appear like she needed to get going. "I, um, should probably get back to it," she said.

"Sure, but take that hike before you do more searching," Meredith said, before getting on her bike and taking off.

Meredith meant well, but Sarith knew her friend didn't really get it. She had never been out of work all that long. She had the type of personality everyone instantly loved and she always got the promotion or the next job and she never really had to think about it.

Sarith wasn't like that. It was a struggle to get any job, but especially ones she wanted the most. And she was getting sick of it.

Now all she had was time to think.

Nine

Sarith rolled over and stretched. The house was quiet again. The clock ticked loudly from the other side of the room. She didn't want to face yet another day, but it was here.

Swinging her legs out of bed, her feet hit the cold floor, and a chill travelled her legs. Winter was coming, and the nights were getting cold. She'd have to put her slippers beside the bed each night. She walked over to the bathroom.

Her time off should have been enjoyable, but each day it was getting harder and harder to get herself out of bed. She didn't want to face another day and entertain questions from people that seemed to only care about jobs and not how she was doing personally.

That morning, she thought about her visit with Meredith. Her words wouldn't stop circling and she knew, even though she didn't love the way Meredith may have said it, that she was right. If she could clear her head and truly think about it all, then maybe it would be easier to decide what to do.

Quickly showering and getting dressed, she looked in the mirror at her worn-out face. It was almost like she could see the wrinkles coming in quick and the circles under her eyes only seemed to deepen in colour over the last few weeks. They acted like accents, highlighting how sunken her face had gotten lately. Sleep wasn't coming easy and for weeks she had hidden it, but as time passed, it was finally showing. Her appetite disappeared and she could barely choke down food at the best of times. She turned to see her profile, then turned back to face her front, running her hands over the sharp collar bones.

Sarith riffled through the jewelry box on her dressing, picking out a necklace, earrings, and a watch Luke had given her back when things were good. She put them on. Maybe if she wore something nice, she would feel less self conscious about the changes happening in her body.

The spot she drove to was where she and Luke had gone hiking years earlier, when Melissa was just a little girl. It was easy, and at the end of it was a gorgeous water-fall they had discovered together.

The path was pretty well worn from years of use, but today there wasn't a single car in the parking lot. She headed up the hill and down the path; the waterfall rum-bling in the distance.

The fall colours caught her eye, and she was in awe of how beautiful the world around her had become and somehow she had missed it. The smell of dried leaves reached her as her feet stirred them up and the sun shone brightly, making her squint. She stopped and took a deep breath. It felt like the world around her was embracing her, like she always belonged out here in the wilderness.

With each step, she felt lighter. She didn't know what she would do next with her life, but at this moment, she was finally at peace.

The longer she was out here, the better she felt. The path wound its way around trees and ponds where frogs sat watching her. She twisted and turned, heading everywhere and nowhere. In the distance, she could hear water roaring and she knew the waterfall was nearby. Finally, she came to it. It was bigger than she remembered. Its roar was loud in her ears. Walking to its edge, she reached her hand out and let the water rush past her fingertips. It was shockingly cold already, but it felt good.

She pushed her hand further in until it covered her wrist. The watch glimmered in the light. She forgot to take it off. Sarith pulled her hand back, but as she did, the watch slipped and fell off onto a rock just behind it.

"Shit," she said, trying to reposition herself to get it. The gold face of it shimmered under the surface. If she could just get closer, maybe she could reach it. She shifted and went to step onto a closer rock. The slimy surface made her foot slip out from under her and, for a moment, she was flailing. She fell through the waterfall and behind it into the water below. The rushing water pushed her deep. Her skin screamed against the cold, instantly erupting into pins and needles. She carefully opened her eyes to see which way was up. Light came to her from somewhere nearby and she pushed herself over to it.

Sarith burst through the cold water and gasped deeply. Her eyes darted back and forth, but the inky sky made it hard to see. A crack of thunder rang out around her and she glanced up just as the sky let go and rain showered down on her. She wiped her face, but the rain made it hard to see.

She swam forward, hoping she would find the shore. Her limbs felt rubbery, and it wouldn't be long before they gave out. She pushed herself, pulling the water past her and soon her legs found soil under them. Relief washed over her as she took each step. As she got closer and the water line receded, she felt her legs give out as the water no longer held most of her weight anymore. Her face fell to the sand, her breaths ragged, and the world went black.

Ten

A crack of thunder echoed through the air.

Sarith jolted awake, her eyes darting around. She sat and looked back at the water behind her and its shiny mercury-like surface swirled and turned like an angry mass. Ahead of her, a forest stretched out in each direction, and further ahead to the left, she could see a mountain, peaking over the tops of the trees. Dark clouds were hovering nearby and the air shifting around her, a chilly breeze making her skin goosebump. The storm was coming in fast.

Her mind raced. Where was she? She had been out on the hike. There was a waterfall, there was her watch. Her watch! She looked down at her bare wrist. Cursing under her breath, she rubbed where it should be. It had fallen off behind the waterfall, and there was no waterfall here. Scanning the shoreline, she didn't see it in the fading light. Her hand searched her neck and ears and she sighed, knowing her other pieces were still there.

The sun would set in about an hour, and she needed to figure out where she was.

Another thunder crackled nearby. Electricity filled the air. She could figure out where she was later. For now, she had to move away from the water, so she headed to the forest. Already, the light wasn't able to penetrate too far in and what came back to her was jagged shadows, making her stomach feel uneasy. But where else could she go?

As if sensing the storm, squirrels skittered up the trees towards their homes; birds landed in their nests and pulled their wings over their young; while a pair of chipmunks ran ahead and disappeared into a small hole in the ground.

More thunder boomed, but this time, it was so close it made her duck. She ran as fast as she could through the undergrowth of the forest, slipping and sliding as the rain poured down around her. Fat raindrops landed on her head and face and she tried to sweep them away to see, but each one felt bigger than the last.

Following the path, she got closer to the mountain until she reached a dark opening in the side of it. Sarith cautiously approached the cave. Normally she would be terrified to go into somewhere like that, but today, she felt nothing. Or maybe it wasn't nothing. It was only a moment, but there was a flickering of feeling that she hadn't felt in so long. She was relieved. It didn't bother her that she was alone, drenched, and hungry. Wherever she was, it wasn't home. And that was enough.

Sarith quickly got in. If nothing else, it would at least keep her dry until she could find something better. Crawling into the corner of the cave, away from the opening, she curled up and closed her eyes. Maybe in the morning, it would be easier to see what was around and could find some answers.

Eleven

Sarith's stomach growled, waking her up out of dead sleep. It had been two days now, and she had found nothing to eat or anyone to ask where she was. The cave had given her shelter, but she knew she had to get herself moving again. The bit of water she had found in a nearby stream had kept her going for now, but she needed some food, and soon.

The sun shone brightly, and the warmth of it felt good. But as the afternoon slipped away, she could feel her anxiety growing. The idea of going to bed hungry yet again terrified her.

Squirrels darted around in front of her as she walked, while birds sang and almost seemed to follow her. She got lost in her thoughts and without realizing it, she was humming along with them. It helped a bit with her nerves. If they could find something to eat, then surely she could too.

A chipmunk darted across her path, carrying a piece of bread.

Didn't they normally eat nuts? She thought to herself as she stopped. Instead of chasing it though, she looked the way it had come. As the trees parted in front of her, she stepped out into a clearing. In the centre was a fire pit with logs surrounding it for sitting. Long sticks leaned up against the seats, the ends charred. Someone had been cooking with them. She stopped singing, but the song continued around her. She shook her head. There was no way she was still hearing it. Was she really that hungry?

She scanned the area. If the chipmunk had found something, then maybe she would too. She was so hungry she almost thought she could still smell something. She raced around the fire and found little tables beside the seats. The first one had nothing. Then the second, nothing. Each spot was empty. She turned to the last one. There, sitting on a small plate, was a leftover crust from a piece of bread. The crust must have been sitting out for quite a while, as it was dried out, but she didn't care. She bit into it as best as she could, gnawing at it with only crumbs breaking off of it.

Sarith sat down on the nearby seat and turned away from the fire. She would keep along the path, heading even further away from the mountain. She hadn't dared venture that far from the comfort of the cave, but as supplies dwindled, she knew she had to move into the unknown.

"I don't see why I have to be the one to clean this up," a voice said behind her. She stood, spinning, and held back a scream. Emerging out of the treeline was a tall, black gorilla with shiny fur that barely covered his large muscular torso. "I was out here for only five minutes last night..."

The gorilla tossed whatever it was in his hands into the fire pit that was only ashes now. It created a little cloud that wafted up and he stopped to watch it before his eyes landed on her.

Sarith didn't know much about gorillas, only the little bits she had experienced at the zoo with her daughter. Usually they were friendly when she had contact with them before, but she knew they could also turn violent. She took a step back, her breath catching in her throat as she watched it.

The gorilla took another step towards her, and she wanted to move away, but fear ran through her. Her feet felt glued in place. Another step. Sarith watched, ready to defend herself. The crust she held fell to the ground. Her eyes darted to it, but remained still.

The gorilla scanned her up and down and then to where she had just looked. He saw the crust on the ground and slowly he reached into a bag slung across his back. Sarith held up her hands and kicked the crust over to him. Maybe if she gave the piece to him, he would leave her alone. He continued to reach into his bag and pulled something out. She felt panic wash over her and just as she was about to run, she saw he had grabbed a sandwich and was unwrapping the paper around it.

"Hungry?" he asked, carefully setting it down before taking a big step back.

"Starving," she said. She eyed him warily, but the hunger was too much. Carefully, she snuck forward and snatched it up before taking a few steps away from him. Flipping the sandwich over, she saw it was peanut butter and jelly made with soft, fluffy bread. She took a big bite. The peanut butter was so fresh it had to be handmade.

"Thank goodness you were here or else I would have starved. Funny how things like this work out sometimes," she said, losing her thoughts in the deliciousness of the sandwich. Sarith stopped for a moment and laughed around the huge bite of sandwich in her mouth. She was talking to a gorilla. There was no way he would understand her. She paused and held the sandwich up.

"Here's to being so hungry you think you're talking to a gorilla."

"You are," he said, moving towards the seat next to the one she had been using earlier.

She stopped chewing, her mouth dropping open. A piece of bread fell out of it before it occurred to her she was gawking. She shook her head and took a step back.

"What?" she asked, the sandwich slipping from her hands. It fell to the ground with a thud and they both stood there looking at each other for a moment. She took a step back, unsure what she should do. But the sandwich had been delicious, and she definitely needed to eat. And it wasn't attacking her. He reached down for it, brushed it off, and held it out to her.

She hesitantly reached to get it.

"I'm not going to attack you," he said. "Usually gorillas will only attack when they feel threatened and I'm handing you food. I clearly don't feel threatened, although I will say I'm very curious about you. I've never seen anything like you before." He motioned for her to do the same. She sat carefully, never taking her eyes off him.

"Where did you come from?" he asked, handing her a container of water.

She took a drink and cleared her throat.

"I'm not actually sure how I got here." She thought back to the waterfall and rubbed her wrist, the missing watch somehow feeling more of a distant memory than before. "There was water, and I think I fell. I ended up finding a cave. I've been sleeping in there the last few days."

"I know the spot," the gorilla said. "But you had to have come from somewhere else? Like, what kind of animal are you?"

"Animal? I'm not an animal," she said, quizzically.

"Then, what are you?"

"Well, I'm human."

The gorilla stopped. "You're human? Like an actual human?"

"Yes," she said, laughing nervously.

"Like, that has dreams?"

"Yes, I've had dreams. Why do you ask?"

"Wow. I can't wait to tell the others!" he said, his eyes lighting up.

"What do you mean?"

"We've never actually seen a human before! This is incredible!" he exclaimed. "I was actually wondering if they even existed!"

"Well, we do…" she said, letting her voice trail off.

"Have you gone very far from the cave?"

"Not really, but I needed food."

"I should probably introduce myself. I'm Darrian Barabus, but everyone just calls me Barabus." He put out his hand to shake hers. She took it and returned the shake.

"I'm Sarith."

"So, if you've been staying in the cave, you're probably out of food, and only having the stream to drink from."

"Yeah. You really do know the spot."

"I do. Listen, I need to do some work around here before I can head home. If you give me a hand cleaning this up for a bit, you can come for dinner and have a proper meal, some hot tea, and even get you a change of clothing."

"That would be great," Sarith said before taking another bite of her sandwich.

Barabus motioned for her to sit.

"I'll get started while you eat." He pulled an apple and some cut up veggies and handed them to her. "Once you're ready, we'll get the rest of this mess cleaned up and we'll be on our way."

Twelve

James crouched in the front garden and pushed the dirt around a plant with his paws. Last night's storm had made the weaker plants come loose, and he wanted to get them taken care of before too long. He took a deep breath as the smell of fresh earth and the lingering smell of rain hung in the air. His body relaxed and the stresses of the last week were finally fading. Being in the garden was the one place that gave him that. There were no rules to it. He could create whatever he wanted. The entire backyard was a labyrinth of flowers, grasses, and cobblestone walkways. If he could dream it, he made it. But this garden was different. This one he kept simple because that's what his mom would have loved. James and his father had made it in her memory.

He got up, stretching his paws up and ran one through his golden fur. Not that it would make a difference. Being a golden retriever, it just rested whatever way it wanted. His mind drifted to his dad. He would have been proud of this garden. The tulips that flowered whenever his dad felt blue, and the marigolds that the honeybees loved stealing nectar from.

He had lost his mom on the journey to this new land. Even though he knew they had to come, he still was dealing with the pain of leaving her behind, buried in a field off the path they had taken. The idea of it still gave him anxiety attacks. They should have brought her back with them to be buried alongside his father.

But James had taken solace in the fact his dad Miguel was here for him. They spent the rest of the journey talking and sharing memories that now meant the world to him. They had grown closer than James had ever remembered them being before. Rather than shutting down and hiding his feelings, his dad had encouraged him to express them, knowing it was the best way to handle them.

At first, the pain had been so deep he didn't know how his heart could still beat, but as the days went on, it turned to anger. How could his mom be gone? Why did it have to be her? He blamed the townsfolk. They should have stayed in their previous home and fought off the hyenas, but they didn't and now his mom was gone and never coming back. And no matter how much he yelled and cried, his dad was always there for him. They had grown inseparable.

So, when his dad started coughing after the first month of being here, James immediately worried. Miguel put up a fight to go see the doctor, even though Miguel and the doctor were good friends, so James had the doctor come to them. It took a few tests, but the same illness that had killed his mother was now in his father. They moved him to a separate room in the hopes of it not spreading, but the illness, whatever it was, ended up taking his father, anyway. The loss hit him like a tsunami. He no longer had his dad to share his feelings with. His friends offered, but no one else had lost both parents in such a short time. They didn't understand the hurricane of emotions that threatened to overwhelm and sink him every day.

James stood and walked away from the garden and into the forest. He hadn't planned it, but as he walked across the uneven ground, he knew where his feet were taking him: his father's final resting place. The stone was a simple one, flat with the ground. It had his dad's name and date of death, but at the bottom it read Beloved Husband, Father and Friend. Writer of Dreams.

It had only been a month since his father died and even though everyone told him the pain would dull over time, his heart still felt raw. Memories came and pierced him like the jagged rock at his father's gravesite. Even though thinking of his dad caused him so much pain, every memory felt like a precious jewel that he desperately clung to.

Now that his father was gone, James knew what it meant for him. It would be on him to take over the dream-writing room. Supervising the dreams was a time-honoured tradition. His father had taken over for his father and his father had before that. He knew he would have to do it, but he just didn't think it would come this early. Now that the time had come, it felt like too much. He didn't want this role to be his life. His heart was in gardening: to spend hours in the dirt, creating and growing gardens unlike anything they had seen before.

Behind him, he felt the rush of air and the flapping of wings as an eagle landed behind him. Alexander had been keeping an eye on him since his father had passed, and he pretty much always knew where James was.

"I thought you'd be here," Alex said, glancing at the stone.

"Nowhere else to go," James said, defeated.

"We need to talk about something," Alex said, turning his gaze to him; pain etched into the depths of his eyes. As much as Alex didn't want to have to start this conversation now, he knew he had to. "I need to show you how to do the supervising."

James took a breath and as he did, Alex saw the tears that threatened to unload from James's eyes but he swallowed them down deep and disappeared somewhere Alex couldn't see.

"I need more time," James said, the pain hitting him again.

"I know. But we don't have much more."

James took a few steps away.

Alex walked alongside him for a few moments before turning to him. James climbed on his back and grabbed hold of his feathers. They took off into the air; the wind rushing through James's fur and momentarily distracting him from everything. It was a different world up here and for a few moments, everything felt possible. Then, the half-constructed castle came into view and reality hit once again.

Whether or not he was ready, his new reality was here.

* * *

Alex landed and James hopped off. The castle was ahead of them and today, with its tall towers, it seemed especially daunting. He had seen the castle many times before; he had practically lived there before his dad's passing, but today, knowing his father wouldn't be in there, dread washed over him. Alex put a wing around him and took them inside.

The hammering of thousands of typewriter keys echoed through the halls. They stopped outside the main room. The smell of typewriter oil burned his nose.

"You've got this," Alex said to him.

Before they entered, they stopped at a table outside the room and opened a drawer. Inside were headsets they both put on before Alex opened the door, entering first.

The room seemed bigger than he remembered. As they entered, a few animals stopped and acknowledged him, but most were busy with their work.

The animals sat at long tables, covered in typewriters. Each one of them was typing away, the keys slapping the thick ivory paper. Two tables over, a rabbit pulled its paper out of the typewriter, and took it over to a table at the far end. The paper was put on top of a pile of others. The rabbit returned to its chair and put a new piece of paper in the typewriter to start the next one.

"I know you understand most of the job already. I'm sure your dad already told you about it, but I want to let you know this is a huge responsibility. And I know it's not the same, but I will be with you every step of the way.

"The main thing is to make sure the writers have everything they need. You will get the data sheets about each person and you will distribute them out to the animals. From there, they write the dreams which make humans have them, but you will walk around and confirm they have everything they need from typewriter tape, to fresh paper, to snacks and water.

"Most of the time, the animals will deliver their sheets to the enchanted boxes after they finish them, but there are some who don't. I usually go around and get their pages."

James followed Alex as he walked over to a nearby giraffe and gave it a quick pat on the back. Beside him was a large stack of typed dreams. He said something to the giraffe, but James couldn't hear it over the sounds of the typewriters. Then he picked up the pile and walked it over to the enchanted boxes. James followed and watched as Alex lifted the lid and put the pile in it, and closed the lid. Alex opened it again a moment later, and it was empty.

James had seen the boxes before, but didn't know how they worked. Seeing the paper missing now surprised him.

"One thing your dad probably wouldn't have gone over with you is where to get the human's data sheets and where you take the dreams afterwards. Follow me."

Alex walked through the room and back towards the entrance. They deposited the headset back in the cupboard and walked down the hall. The sound of the typewriters faded as they turned the corner and away from the room.

They stopped near the end of the hall and Alex opened a door.

He stepped back and let James enter first.

"What's this?" James asked, almost breathless.

"This is the mail room," Alex said, beaming.

* * *

Before them lay a room, the front of it dominated by a long counter. The walls featured gold tubes that ran down from the ceiling and slanted toward the middle. Animals walked back and forth, carrying cylinders to different parts of the room. James stopped, eyes scanning.

"Clearly, you haven't seen this before," Alex said to him as he walked ahead of James and went to lean on the glass counter.

"What is this place?" he asked, finally finding his footing and joining Alex.

"Well, like I said, it's the mailroom. These cylinders have sheets of paper in them that tell us about the humans. It gives us details about their hopes, dreams, and ambitions that help us write dreams to inspire or at least bring encouragement."

"Did we have these in the last place?" James asked, never remembering his dad even talking about this room before.

"We did. We had brought the cylinders and angled part of the tubes, and well, the magic did the rest."

James watched as another golden retriever reached into an enchanted box for a typed dream and rolled it up. They opened the end of a golden cylinder and slipped the paper inside. Then they replaced the lid and put it in a golden tube and James could hear it being pulled away to some-where else.

"Maybe he was waiting for the right timing," Alex said, motioning for James to follow him. "So the cylinders on the left wall here are for the info pages coming to us. Someone empties them each day and puts the paper into one of the enchanted boxes we take to the dream writers.

"The wall on the right is for dreams once they are typed. They get put into a cylinder and then are taken away."

"What happens after that?"

"I suspect someone stores them somewhere."

"You don't know?"

"No one really knows." Alex showed him to the other side of the room so he could watch as the cylinders were emptied and the pages placed in an enchanted box, which Brownie, the large chocolate brown moose, and another moose were taking them on their backs toward the dream writing rooms.

"Let's go back to the dream-writing rooms," Alex said, heading down another hallway.

"So, this is the room your father supervised, but what you don't know is there are many more rooms he was just about to take over."

"What? I thought everyone only did one?" James said, feeling a wave of anxiety washing over him.

"Well, your dad was one heck of a guy," Alex smiled. "When he first started talking about it at a town council meeting, we weren't so sure, but after watching him with the writers, we knew he could handle it. But before we could do so, the move happened. Council said once every-thing was here and set up again, that we would tell him. But, well, you know the rest."

James's eyes dropped to the floor between his paws.

"I know this is all a lot to process, but after losing your father, we are having several of his coworkers supervising his room and they can't handle the responsibility of it long term.

"Now, we're not expecting you to do that, taking on as much as he was going to, but it was always the plan for you to follow suit and at least supervise one room. And who knows, maybe you'll get so good you can take on more than one like your dad wanted to do. There's no rush for that, though."

James lifted his eyes to Alex and could feel the room swirling around him. He couldn't focus on anything and he felt like he was going to be sick. He reached out beside him and grabbed an empty chair and stumbled into it.

"James, I'm sorry. I shouldn't have gone into all that. It's just we need to train you soon. This is your future and we want to help you get there," Alex said, coming over and placing a wing on his arm.

James looked up at him again and shook the wing off. His vision cleared, and he felt like he finally could see clearly.

"So, you want me to just give up any dreams I had and just… come do what you expect, even though I don't want to?"

"Well…" Alex said, letting his words fall away.

"I'm not doing this. This is too much!" James rushed to the door and threw it open. From down the hall, he could hear the typing, so he turned and ran. He wasn't ready for this. He didn't want this future. This had been his dad's life and he wasn't ready to step into it. How could he be when his heart still felt as raw as a fresh wound that still needed to be stitched up?

"James, wait!" Alex said, pushing the door open behind him.

James didn't look back. He went down the next hall and towards the main doors of the castle and raced outside. This was all too much and he wasn't about to let anyone tell him what he needed to do. He was the one in charge of his own future and they were crazy to think that he was just going to do whatever they wanted him to do.

He ran and ran, wanting to be as far away from this place as he could.

* * *

James ran until he felt like his lungs were going to explode. He didn't stop until he finally realized where he was going: back towards his dad's grave. It didn't seem to matter how many times he said he would not come back here, he always returned. Somehow here he felt closest to this dad.

He felt the anxiety rushing through his veins as he thought everything through. James took a few deep breaths, but with each breath, he only got more anxious. He had no idea how he was going to do this and the realization that this was now his job was almost too much to bear.

James's head dropped. Fresh tears fell to the ground and struck the top of his father's grave. The stone turned dark grey where the tear hit and soaked into it. He opened his eyes again, tracing the letters engraved on it. His dad's entire life had been letters and now that's all that's left. He didn't want this job. He didn't want this life. He wanted more than just words and letters. He wanted to make his mark on this world. Some people saw gardening as a temporary thing, but not when you create full forests with trees that last for hundreds of years.

He wiped his eyes and moved his paws around the stone. He would create a bonsai tree. It was one of his dad's favourites. He closed his eyes and put his paw out, picturing the thing slowly coming out of the ground and the trunk getting thicker. The flowers he would make deep red; his dad's favourite colour.

When James reopened his eyes, he moved his paw and instead of being a flowering tree, it was nothing but ash.

He tried again and again, but nothing came up. Instead, the grass around it was turning dark and ashy.

His ears pulsed with heat. He was so angry he couldn't stand it. He slammed his fist down on his father's gravestone. Immediately, he heard it crack. He lifted his paw, blood trickling down, and one drop swelled on his fur for a moment before finally falling onto the stone below. The air chilled suddenly and he shivered. The ashes flew up from the ground, swirling around him before blowing behind a nearby maple tree.

He waved his paw over the stone again. It came together and sealed itself, but James could still see where it had cracked. It shouldn't be like that. Magic never left a negative mark on things. He tried again, but it stayed there. He took a deep breath and took a few steps away from his dad's stone. Now there was a permanent reminder of his anger. James staggered back a few more steps, bumping into the maple tree that gave his dad's place shade and shelter. He looked down and saw that his paws were shaking. He tried again to seal the stone, but it didn't change.

He went to leave, but as he did, he stumbled over something. A small animal sat at his feet and looked up at him with the darkest eyes that James had ever seen. James stepped back and it let out a small growl that made him laugh.

"Where did you come from?" he asked, as he slowly crouched. James didn't recognize what animal it was. It had a small body, with a slightly larger head, and was covered with black fur that was almost too long.

It tilted its head to the side and let its tongue fall out. It panted and tried to take a few steps, but it stumbled and fell.

"Do you have a mom around here?" James asked it, even though he was certain it didn't have any idea where it was or what he was saying.

It tried to walk again, but stumbled.

"I can't exactly leave you here, now can I? You can't even get yourself to water," James said.

He picked it up and walked away. He had to get his animal back to his place and try to figure out how to take care of it. Now felt like the worst time to take on something else, but maybe this was the very thing he needed to keep himself distracted from the things to come.

* * *

The forest where James had been was silent, except a small whimper. From behind the tree near the gravestone, a small grey squirrel scurried out, stumbling as it went. He righted himself and glanced around. The sounds of James and the other creature that had been with him were now gone, making him feel all alone. Walking away from where the sun shone, he made his way through the forest. He didn't know where he was going, but he bounced along. He so badly wanted to climb a tree, but each time he tried, he slid back down. Maybe when he got bigger, he would make that climb. He wanted to see the world around him. Already it looked huge. He could only imagine what he would see up that high.

Another time, he thought. He stopped when he needed to. He ate when he found food and little by little he made his way. Where he was going, he didn't know but he loved the journey.

Thirteen

Sarith had never worked alongside a gorilla before, yet somehow they seemed to fall into a rhythm together. He showed her where the waste needed to go and she gathered it up, while he worked on putting the chairs back in the right spots and tidying up the fire pit. She watched him for a moment and somehow it seemed like he could make changes faster than she could keep up. She couldn't understand how he worked so fast.

As the sunlight faded to twilight, Barabus helped her pick up the last few forgotten things.

"Well, that took us longer than expected," Sarith said, following Barabus back to the path. But instead of heading straight into the forest, they turned right. Sarith lost all sense of direction as they went, but she knew they weren't heading towards the mountain. Even at this time of day, the air felt warmer as they left the shelter of the mountain and the cool air that came down from the peak.

"It was quite the party," Barabus said. "I'm surprised you didn't hear it."

"Once I fell asleep, I was out," she said.

"Well, we'll have a proper meal and maybe some wine?" Barabus said, a twinkle in his eye.

"That would be great," she said, laughing. She didn't know what this place was, but so far, she really liked it.

* * *

The squirrel bounced along the path in the woods, listening to all the other creatures around him. He wanted to say hi, but he felt so shy.

Maybe tomorrow.

The light was fading and he needed to find somewhere to stay for the night. He had found a squirrel path and had followed it most of the day. It ran alongside another path that was wider and more packed down. He almost moved over, but two voices carried in the wind, making him nervous. When they came into view, he hid behind a tree. One was furry like him, but one wasn't. She had long hair and was dressed differently than the other. But even that wasn't the most confusing part. The one with the longer hair had a light trailing behind her, almost like it was following her. No, it was coming out of her. Or off of her? He wasn't sure, but he definitely saw it. The little squirrel decided to stay hidden for now. What if that light wasn't friendly? He couldn't risk it just yet.

Fourteen

"It's not much, but here it is," Barabus said as they came up to a small home at the far end of town.

"Thanks for letting me stay with you," she said as she took a step inside. The home suddenly seemed twice as big as it had from the outside. There was a kitchen and dining area just inside the doorway with a hallway leading off to rooms beyond.

"My room is just down the hall on the left. You can have the room on the right. Bathroom is at the end of the hall."

"That's great," she said, taking it all in. She walked over to the kitchen where a banana tree grew in the one corner, with all the bunches at different stages in their growth.

"A banana tree?" she laughed.

"It's my favourite food. And there's nothing like a fresh-ly picked banana."

He walked over and pulled one of the yellow ones off and pulled back part of the peel and handed it to her. "You're not allergic, are you?"

She shook her head and took a bite. It wasn't just a good banana. It was the best banana she had ever had before. It was creamy with a much stronger flavour than any of the bananas at home had ever been. She hadn't thought of home all day. It seemed strange that she hadn't, but she didn't want to think about that now. She took another bite.

"Glad you like it," he said, taking one for himself.

"So, should we talk about the one thing that we really haven't discussed?"

"Which is…?" she asked before finishing the banana and throwing the peel in a compost pail she found underneath the sink.

"Well, you came here from somewhere else."

"Yes."

"And you said you remember some water? Did you come in through a lake?"

"I think maybe? I'm not really sure," she said, picking at the cuticle on her left thumb.

"I wonder if we should try and maybe find a way for you to get home."

"It all seems like so long ago. It might actually have been through a cave, or was it…" she said, as a piece of cuticle came off and blood trickled down her nail. Using her pointer finger, she pressed down on the sore and let her hands drop but kept on the pressure. "I'm not even sure if I remember anymore. I don't even know how long I was out there wandering around before you found me." But even as she said it, she wasn't sure if he would actually believe her or not. She certainly didn't sound very convincing in her ears. Of course she remembered the lake is where she came in, but she wasn't ready to go home already. She wanted to see more about this magic and what it all meant. And if there was any chance, she wondered if she had some magic herself.

Barabus looked at her, but she could tell he didn't fully believe her. Sarith tried not to blush and turned towards the bedroom.

"I'm pretty tired, and a night's sleep in an actual bed sounds great," she said, faking a yawn.

"Of course."

Just as she put her hand on the doorknob, he called back to her. "You'll let me know when you remember more, though, right?"

"Yeah. Sure," she said, closing the door. Only if this world ended up being dangerous, would she decide to leave, but for now, she wasn't going anywhere.

Fifteen

The morning sunlight was bright in her room. Sarith had walked into the bedroom the night before and hadn't even looked around. She had just seen the bed and let herself slide under the covers. The mattress was as soft as a cloud and she had fallen into a peaceful and dreamless sleep that, when she woke up the next morning, she felt like a week had passed.

She opened the door to the smell of toast with peanut butter and bowls of fruit. A teapot sat on the stove, steam coming out of the spout.

"Freshly made," Barabus said as he grabbed a second mug and filled it. He passed it to her and she happily took it. She looked around for milk and sugar but didn't see any.

"How much?" he asked.

"Huh?"

"Milk and sugar. It's almond milk. I hope that's ok."

"Oh, that's fine. Just a splash of each."

Barabus nodded and sat down in his chair, taking a sip of his own. Sarith looked around, confused, but then the cup of tea caught her eye. Milk was in it now, and it swirled as if someone had just stirred it. She put the cup down and took a step back.

"How did you do that?" she asked, wiping her face.

"Magic is a wonderful thing," he said, raising an eyebrow.

She hesitantly took her mug over to the chair beside him and sat, taking a sip. It was made absolutely perfectly, and she loved the moment of quiet to start the day.

Barabus flicked his wrist and the plates that were already filled with food floated over to them and gently landed on their laps.

Breakfast was the best she had had in years. Somehow it tasted fresher and better than anything she'd had at home.

"I need to go back into town. Hey," he said, like he finally remembered something, "why don't you come with me? You can see how things work, and maybe you can lend a hand at some point?"

"That sounds great. I'd love to help, if that's ok," she said. "I have some experience and I'm actually pretty good at building things."

"Well, it's not really up to me, but we can ask," Barabus said. "It's up to Terrance. He's the mayor. I'll introduce you."

She followed Barabus out the door. She didn't want to admit it, but she was excited to see what they could do.

* * *

The grey squirrel bounced along again after a full night's rest. It had found the most perfect hole to crawl into at the base of a tree. It was warm and cozy and after a full day of walking and searching out his new area, he was more than ready to rest.

When the first morning light shone across the horizon, the squirrel was ready to start the day. He tried again to climb a tree and as he reached up, grabbing the next branch was easier today than the day before, almost like he was already bigger. It took some time, but he got to the top, and carefully scurried out on one of the branches. He inched his way along until he was right at the end of it. The branch dipped as it held his weight and swayed as he moved up and down, up and down. Across an opening, he saw another branch not far off that he wanted to reach. Up and down, up and down.

With a little bit of strength and courage, he jumped as the branch reached its highest point. He flew through the air and spied a branch. It was below him and as long as he didn't move too far in either direction, he would reach it.

He slowed to a stop and gravity brought him back down. He watched the branch rush up towards him and he reached out for it. He grabbed and continued downwards as the branch absorbed his weight, then flung back up. He held tight and even though he thought he couldn't hold on, he did and as the branch soon started to right itself, he carefully walked towards the tree trunk and out towards the next branch. Jumping from branch to branch was fast and soon he saw something curious. Shelters made out of stones and clay came into view with other animals going in and out of them. He even saw some animals moving rocks around like they were making these structures.

Not far from the building was the one figure from the day before that he had seen but she no longer glowed.

He climbed down and walked along the ground. He heard laughing in the distance. And something ahead smelt really good. It was nutty and fruity and it made his stomach growl. He approached the building area carefully, avoiding the walls they were putting up. He would scurry across the open area and head straight for that lovely smelling food.

Hopefully they wouldn't mind sharing.

Sixteen

Barabus and Sarith walked down the dirt road, and towards the part of town they were working on. After all the days of walking alone through the forest, it was nice to finally have someone to be with. The trees weren't as thick here and sunshine shone through, lighting their path.

The surrounding sounds were different than they had been for the last few days. Here it was quieter but almost more uniform. If she didn't know any better, she would also swear that she heard the same thing over and over: the word "new."

"We only moved here a few months ago, so the town isn't complete yet, but everyone has been pitching in," Barabus said, walking beside her.

"What made you come here?"

"In our last land, we were running out of water. We had been searching for a new home for months, and heard about a place that had the freshest water anyone could ask for, but it was far. Almost too far. But we needed to go. Hyenas were closing in and we were in danger. One night, they attacked and drove us out and took some of our leaders. We tried to rescue them, but it didn't work out.

"After that happened, we left. We travelled as far west as we could until we thought we couldn't go any further. Then we found this place, and well, that's the gist of it. Since arriving, we've been working on building ourselves a home."

They headed down the second street and Sarith saw the rest of the townsfolk ahead gathered in groups, each one working on something different.

All eyes immediately flicked to them. It made her feel so awkward, but most of them appeared almost happy to see her. She didn't love it at first, but with each step, it grew on her. There was something about the attention that made her feel important.

"This place hasn't seen a human before. This is all new to us," Barabus said, leaning towards her as they walked.

They went to the centre of town and stopped. There were a few homes around the square and some on streets branching off. Animals walked up and down the street, some working on the gardens in front of the homes, while others were working on stores, a pub, and an art gallery.

A lion stood off to the left and motioned to a few other animals around him. Sarith stopped short. She had never been this close to a lion before and the sight of it, with its large mane and sharp teeth, made her legs weak.

Barabus walked ahead, but quickly noticed she wasn't following. He turned back and saw her there, frozen in place. He followed her eyeline and saw that she was staring at the lion and walked back over to her.

"Everything ok?" he asked, watching the lion talking with the others.

"I've never been so close to a lion before," she whispered, a tremor in her voice.

"He's friendly, if that's what you're concerned about," Barabus said, smiling. He motioned for her to follow him to another group of animals, slowly moving rocks in place to build a home. Sarith watched for a moment before she realized they weren't working that hard. Somehow, they weren't even breaking into a sweat. She got closer, standing right beside a great dane, and watched. The boulders were moving by themselves. She couldn't understand it. How could they be doing that?

"Guys, come meet someone," Barabus called out to his friends. All around her, animals came over and surrounded her. Most were surprised. "This is Sarith."

The animals eyed her with such wonderment and a bit of apprehension. But if she was the first human they ever saw, she could understand it.

"She wants to help build the town," Barabus said to Terrance, but Sarith could see he was unsure.

"I'm not sure what all I can do, but I would love to try," Sarith said, trying to sound as confident as possible.

Terrance nodded, and he motioned for everyone to get moving along. As they dispersed, he turned to the two of them.

"Now, we don't have much in the way of tools and whatnot. A lot of this is done with magic, but if you want to try, that's no problem. Maybe you can help move things in place to start."

Sarith went with Barabus over to a home that only had two walls up and no roof. She was shown where the stones were coming from and she walked over and started moving them, one at a time. Barabus watched her for a moment and stepped back. He put out his arms towards the pile and closed his eyes. A moment later, two blue beams of light hit the pile of rocks beside where Sarith was grabbing from. She jumped back and her eyes followed the path to Barabus's hands. She watched as they lifted a rock over her head and swung around towards the home. He put it on the line that the others had made, where the third wall would be. With one hand still held up, he moved the other hand, which made one stone at a time drop into place. Once they were all level, he walked over and inspected their placement. Someone else was already moving more in and he stepped back and let them finish.

None of this seemed real.

"How are they doing that?" she asked.

"You've never seen magic before?"

"I've seen magic before and it's always just a sleight-of-hand kind of thing. It's not real."

"Sleight-of-hand? What does that mean?" Barabus asked, but before she could answer, the pack of dogs that had been working on the one wall stepped aside and a flock of seagulls came in with a roof. Thick wires suspended it below them. They carefully lowered it down and, once in position, the pack moved back in and unclipped it. The birds flew off and Sarith assumed it was to get another roof. The pack held out their arms, and a moment later, the seam between the roof and the walls filled with thick clay and almost instantly it was drying.

Something that would have taken days to build in her land was done in moments and in ways that made no sense to her.

"You want to try, don't you?" Barabus said, smiling.

"What do I have to do?"

"Well, usually, we have to think about something that makes us happy. That will get it started. Once that thought is in us, then we can start using the magic to work for us. I think about what I want the magic to do, so in this case, I want to make the wall for this home. I will picture the rocks, moving up and over to the place where they are going to land."

Sarith took a deep breath and held out her hands like she had just seen Barabus doing. She closed her eyes and tried to think of something that made her happy. In a moment, her daughter came to mind. She could picture her as a young girl, happy, laughing, enjoying herself, and having fun. Melissa had been such a sweet girl. Sarith had loved watching her learn as a toddler. She felt something in her at that moment. She opened her eyes and looked at the pile of rocks. From her hands, she could see red sparks starting. She threw her hands down to her side and watched as the sparks and red beams hit the ground at her feet. She jumped back and put her hands out. The beams were still hitting the ground, but the grass under them was swirling. Barabus yelled over the rushing in her ears to point to the rock pile, so she did. Moving her hands up, the beams went all over. Animals dodged out of the way and backed up. A few looked concerned, but Sarith hardly noticed. All of her attention was on the boulder at the top of the pile. It was moving. It started just as a tremor at first, but soon it was up in the air and she carefully tried to move it towards them and the wall. She let herself drift back to thinking about Melissa: her first steps, first words, first foods. But as quickly as the good things came to her mind, the last few years of trouble disrupted them. Melissa had got mixed in with the wrong crowd and came home many nights either too late, drunk, or high.

"Sarith!" Barabus said, his hands going up.

"What?" she asked, but she had lost track of what she was doing. The rock had flown up high into the air, and was swinging back and forth erratically. Sarith moved her hands down, but overdid it and the rock smashed into the ground, creating an enormous crater and making every-thing shake around them. A grey squirrel stood beside it stunned, nearly getting crushed by the boulder. Everyone darted back from the scene. Terrance came running over.

"What happened?" he asked, seeing the rock that was half buried in the ground.

"Sorry. I'm… sorry," she muttered, shoving her hands deep into her pockets.

"Don't worry about it," Barabus said, putting an arm around Terrance and leading him back over to the home and away from Sarith.

She couldn't hear what they were saying, but she could tell that Barabus was trying to sweet talk him. She slowly approached the frightened squirrel that remained where it was, shaking in fear.

"I'm sorry," she said. Sarith sat down beside it and it took a few steps towards her, but stopped. "I didn't mean to nearly hurt you. I didn't know what was going on. I got lost in thought again."

The squirrel came over to her and crawled onto her lap. She gave it a gentle pat, and it nuzzled into her hand. He was clearly young, and he appeared almost too thin. He needed food. She stood. Terrance motioned for everyone to get back to work. He did a quick wave to Sarith and went around the other side and started work on the fourth wall.

"What did you say to him?" Sarith asked once Barabus returned.

"Oh, I just told him not to worry about it, amongst other things. He said he'll let me take care of things. Who's that you have there?" Barabus asked, seeing the squirrel in her hands.

"I don't know. He's the one that almost got crushed by the rock. He's so young and too thin. I think we need to get him something to eat."

Barabus grabbed a few snacks from the snack area nearby and put them out towards the squirrel. The squirrel quickly grabbed the container of nuts and tried to yank off the lid. Sarith gently took it, pried off the lid, and returned it. The squirrel ate and almost looked like he was smiling.

"Does he have a name?" Barabus asked. Sarith and the squirrel both shrugged.

The words from a book Sarith had been reading before she came here ran through her head.

"What about Woodrow?" she asked. The squirrel scurried around her, happily. "I guess that's it then." She gave his head another scratch.

"I can take care of him," Cynthia, a white rabbit said, walking over. Sarith handed him over before turning to ask Barabus more, but he was already walking towards the rock she had flung into the ground.

The pack of dogs had joined Barabus, trying to get the rock out. But they needed to add another dozen folks before they saw even a hint of movement from it. Long minutes passed before they managed to get out of the hole and onto the flat ground beside it.

Barabus took a deep breath and held out his hands. The rock moved easily now that it was out of the ground, and he brought it over to the wall and placed it carefully on top.

Sarith couldn't help but notice the confusion on his face when he came back over to her.

"What's up?" she asked.

"Well, that was just strange. It took all of us to get it out of the ground, something I should have been able to do myself. Then, moving it over to the wall, I could do it on my own..." His voice trailed off.

"No matter. Maybe just try smaller stones for now," Barabus said, taking a step away from her towards the wall. The others were murmuring to each other, and he went over to join them. After a few moments and words that Sarith couldn't hear, they finally went back to work. A few of them looked over their shoulders at her, and she smiled at them. They returned a bit of a forced smile and got themselves working again.

Something about their reaction sat strange with her, but she shrugged it off. It was her first actual attempt. She'd get this figured out.

Seventeen

Sarith worked the rest of the day, moving one rock at a time with her bare hands. Only when she had moments alone did she try using magic again. She held her hands out and tried balancing a rock midair, but keeping it steady felt nearly impossible. Every moment she had to focus with everything in her just to keep it steady. She would try to walk the stones over to the house, but each time it shot off in other directions, sometimes nearly hitting the others working nearby. A few noticed, but most stayed focused on the task at hand.

As the sun got lower in the sky, Terrance called out that it was time to go home.

"We did so much today!" Sarith said, feeling tired but energized. "Are we doing anything else tonight?"

"Well, sometimes a few of us will gather for a fire and some food. I wasn't sure if you'd want to do that though, so I told the guys I probably wouldn't be there today."

"No, let's go!" she exclaimed.

"Really?" he asked, walking with her over to his home. "Well, we should at least clean up a bit."

They arrived at the house. He opened the door for her as she stepped inside.

"I don't really have anything to change into."

Barabus looked at her like the thought hadn't even occurred to him. He walked over to her room and to the chest of drawers that was in the corner. He closed his eyes for a moment and, even though she didn't see it, she knew something happened.

He opened the door, and inside it was full of gorgeous clothing. He moved out of the way for her to see.

"I guessed on the size, but I'm usually not too far off on that type of thing. And if it is wrong, we can get the seamstress to fix it for us. Refitting is a different kind of magic."

She pulled out a bright teal shirt covered in flowers and a modest neckline. At the bottom of the wardrobe were two piles of pants and a few skirts. She grabbed a fresh pair of blue jeans. She went to thank Barabus, but he was already gone.

Sarith slipped on the clothes, which surprisingly fit perfectly, and met him in the living room. He had freshened up in the bathroom.

Barabus extended his elbow for her to grab and as she hooked her arm through his black furry one, she glanced at him. His eyes sparkled and he beamed with pride. While other animals were looking at her like an oddity, he almost appeared to adore her. It had been so long since she had felt that way, and feeling it again made her happy. She placed her other hand on his.

Maybe being here would be good after all.

Eighteen

They arrived at the fire pit and already it was surrounded. The blaze cast shadows that danced across their faces.

Heads turned as they approached. She tried to smile, but the looks on their faces were hard to read. Beside her, Barabus still had that same adoring look he had when they had left. She liked the way Barabus puffed out his chest with pride, like she was worth something.

Introductions were made all around. There were the fox twins Michael and Anthony; Cynthia, the rabbit whose nose wouldn't stop twitching; Alex an eagle; and Woodrow.

"Tell us about yourself!" Cynthia exclaimed. "We've never actually been around a human like this before! Tell us everything."

Sarith didn't even know where to start, it all felt like a dream or a past life. Luke and her job was an easy place to start. She shared about the stresses. Her face lit up as she talked about Melissa. She was the one person who Sarith missed more than anything. She started to ramble, and then she stopped herself. The folks around her seemed ok with it though.

"I didn't even mean to leave there. I was out for a walk after one of my friends encouraged me to… I had been in a bad headspace, you know? But I went for this walk and was pretty far down the path when—"

"Hey guys," James said, walking into the space around the fire pit.

"James!" Terrance said.

"What took you so long to get here?" he asked, watching as James sat and started to talk.

"Oh you know how things are. Today was quite the day…" James started and the conversation drifted to their lives here.

Sarith watched the animals and was struck by how similar their actions were to humans. They laughed, joked, and talked just like her and her friends but the topics of conversations were different. At home, they talked about bills, stresses of life, and situations she would prefer to forget. Here, however, they talked about the joys of life, the amazing things they had seen that day, and seemed so much happier. There was a lightness to the conversation and to this world that didn't exist where she was from.

Sarith's eyes wandered over each animal around the campfire before finally settling on the flames. She could still remember the last time she was at a campfire. Luke and her hadn't been married all that long and it was with all his college buddies. Sarith didn't like them. Most of them were drunks living off of their parents' money and had no ambition of their own. Luke was different, though.

He had been the first guy that had ever pursued her. He had shown her he wanted to do someone with his life. That was back when he was different. Back then, he didn't want to follow the path his parents had laid out for him. Back then, he didn't seem to fit in with them, yet somehow they were his people.

That night, as the alcohol flowed and their language loosened, Sarith learnt more about Luke than she had before they got married. Luke knew paving his own way was going to be hard, but he never thought it would be this hard. Every time he had to give up something else from his old lifestyle, he became more bitter and angry. He tried to hide the emotions, but was terrible at it. His moods became more erratic.

That night at the fire, he had totally changed. He talked about things in a way that were so different from before. He admitted to considering joining the family business, which wasn't that successful, and trying to turn it around.

But as he talked, Sarith knew that if he did that, he not only would be miserable, but he wouldn't be able to do it. It's not that she didn't believe in him, it was that she knew he wouldn't work as hard as he needed to to make the company work. Until that moment, he had never taken a genuine interest in the business and so his knowledge of it was so little. How could he possibly expect to turn a business around when he had never taken the real time needed to make it happen?

She tried to say something, but he yelled at her to hush as he chugged another beer, before crushing the can under foot and tossing it into the wooded area behind them.

Waves of anger rushed her for being dismissed in front of so many of his friends. Her words felt unimportant and she couldn't stop the rush of heat that flushed her face, and the anger that pierced her mind. She thought she knew this man that sat in front of her, but he never would have done that normally. Crossing her arms, she sat back and listened for the rest of the night. She would talk to him more the next day.

But when the time came, Luke only backpedaled. He said all the things she wanted to hear, but she knew it wasn't sincere. She knew him well enough to know the truth.

Thinking about it only made her angry again. She remembered that feeling so vividly, like it had just happened. Heat flushed her face and anger reached her fingertips. She clenched her fist tight, but she couldn't stop that wave of feeling again.

She focused on the fire trying to calm herself, but as she sat there, staring at the flames, her anger roared and she slammed her fist against her leg. Before her, the fire flared into the sky, lighting up the entire area.

The crowd all jumped back, scared.

"What was that?!" one of them said.

Sarith jumped back too. It was the exact moment she had hit her leg that the fire had flared. But that had to be a coincidence, right?

As the flame died down, the group carefully sat back down. Concern was etched on their faces. She sat and took a deep breath. Thinking about Luke had been what made her anger flare up. He had been such a jerk.

The crowd got back into conversation, but her mind drifted back to Luke. He had taken over the business after that. They, as a couple, had sunk more money into it and just as they were about to close it, it finally started to make money. It was slow, but she could see the stress coming off of him as he saw the accounts getting better. Slowly, he went back to the person she remembered. She hoped that side of him wouldn't reappear, but knew it was only a matter of time.

Her anger rose again. She stared into the flames and tried to control her temper. That had been the first time she saw him for who he really was. The flames before her grew taller. Not as tall as before and she seemed to be the only one that noticed.

The group erupted with laughter, bringing her back to the present. She grinned, pretending like she had heard them. Looking back at the fire, the height of the flames went back down.

James and Alex stood and said some goodbyes as they left the circle. Sarith leaned over to Barabus and asked where they were going.

"They're heading home. James has a full day of dream-writing room supervise training in the morning and he needs to get some rest. Alex has been training him, but there's a lot to learn."

"What's a dream-writing room?"

Barabus scrunched his brows confused, but looked into the fire again. That must have been what they were talking about before, and she missed it.

"I'll show you in the morning. We'll help the crew there do some work on the castle if you're up for it."

"Are you sure you want my help after earlier?" Sarith asked, thinking about nearly crushing Woodrow. She looked over at him and watched as his tail twitched as he talked.

"We all make mistakes. No reason you can't have a second chance."

The room's name sparked her interest. Dreams always fascinated her. Tomorrow couldn't come soon enough.

Nineteen

The sun rose and shone through the open slits of the window curtains. Alex rolled over and immediately threw his feet over the side of the bed. It was time. James kept saying he wasn't ready for this, but they could delay it no longer. Alex could only take on the extra responsibilities of the dream-writing room for so long.

James needed to step up.

He walked to the outer door and out into the fresh air. Taking a deep breath, he flapped his wings. The wind rushed past his feathers and gave him a lift. He took off and watched as the ground disappeared under him. The tops of the trees grew smaller as he sailed higher. In the distance, he could see the lake. Animals surrounded it. It was another favourite spot for the town to socialize. To the east he could see the castle, or what there was of it, sitting in an empty field. Nearby were Barabus and Sarith making their way towards it. He didn't like how close she was getting to the dream-writing room. There was no way a human writing dreams was a good idea. What if it altered more than just the person's dreams? He would have to address that later, but for now, he had somewhere to be.

Turning away, he headed towards the outskirts of town. He swooped down as he neared James's home and saw him outside. James was walking towards the house, but something was following him. From this distance, he couldn't tell what it was, but James let it into his house. Alex landed and saw the door open again.

"Alex, what are you doing here?" James asked, pulling the door closed behind him as he stepped outside.

"We need to talk," Alex said. "Barabus is at the castle with Sarith. They are planning to work there. Since that will eventually be your home, do you want to help them with the setup?"

"You can't make an exception for me to stay here?" James said, thinking about his dad. This was the home they had lived in together. His dad's presence was all over the place. He remembered the day they built it. His dad had custom-built everything from the doorknobs to the layout. He had added walls as their needs changed, and James had worked on the gardens, tending to every inch of it until it was perfect. James had mentioned wanting some-where to sit and enjoy his morning tea, and his dad disap-peared for an hour and came back with a detailed drawing of a gazebo that would sit in the back corner of their yard. Over the next few days, they built it together with each spare moment they had. Since losing his dad, the only place he felt close to him was either his final resting place or in this home. He still sat every morning in that gazebo with a cup of tea in hand. He would talk out loud to his dad, even though he knew he was gone and somehow it softened the deep piercing pain that the absence of his father had left.

"James, I know this is hard… but we only let your dad live here instead of the castle because of you. Every other dream writer has to live closer to the work," he said. "You have to be close to the rooms. You'll still have some time before you need to fully move in. They won't get the rooms all done today, but it will be soon."

James sighed. "You have no idea how hard this is!"

Alex went to step closer to him, but James stepped back. No one knew the pain he was feeling. No one knew what it felt like to lose someone so close to him. It was a pain he knew he would never fully recover from.

"I can give you a ride," Alex said after a while.

"I'd prefer to walk."

Alex knew it would take at least thirty minutes for him to walk, but maybe it would do him good. Instead of arguing, he just took off, leaving James on his own.

* * *

James waited until Alex was out of sight and walked back into the house. The creature bounced over to him. It let James pick it up, and he carried it over towards the fireplace. Placing it on the rug, he went back to the kitchen. He'd give it water and food, leave, and pray it didn't tear the place to shreds.

In the moments when his back was turned, the sound of something tearing reached his ears. He spun. The creature was ripping at a blanket he had over the one chair.

"No!" he yelled, as he ran to it. "Don't do that!" He looked at the blanket. It was the last one that his father had given him before they moved. Heat rose in the back of his neck. He picked the blanket up. The tear was a few inches across and would take at least a few hours to repair properly. This wasn't a repair to make with magic. His dad had made it by hand, and he would do the same with the repair. But even still, it would leave a pretty big scar.

"What is wrong with you?" he screamed. His anger poured out of him and he could feel a tingling sensation rising in the back of his neck. His fingers went numb and his head swirled. He grabbed the chair in front of him to brace himself so he wouldn't fall over. He didn't know how much time passed before he finally opened his eyes again and peered at the small creature in front of him. Taking deep breaths, he rolled his shoulders back and stretched his neck from side to side.

The creature cocked its head to the left and then bounced over the fireplace and played in the ash that covered the hearth.

But James noticed a difference in the creature. It appeared bigger. That couldn't be right.

Anger tingled his ear tips and he closed his eyes. He needed to get these feelings under control. If he could just calm himself down, he would see that the creature wasn't any different.

Turning, he put the blanket into his room, slammed the door, and stormed into the second room. James ripped the blankets off the bed and took anything else out of it he didn't want ruined and put them in his room. He walked over to it; he picked it up and moved it to the secondary bedroom. James grabbed a scrap blanket and put it in the creature's bed. Instantly, it darted over and nuzzled in. Now he was positive it was bigger. He rubbed his eyes and knew he wasn't in a place to figure it out right now. He really should tell someone about this thing, but soon, it felt like every aspect of his life was going to be known as he moved into the castle and moved into his supervisor role. He had seen it with the others. At least his dad being here had given them some privacy.

No, he wouldn't share this just yet. He still had his own space for now, and he would keep this quiet.

As he closed the door to his house, he knew he needed to hustle. Alex was waiting for him, and if he took too much more time, he would have to answer questions he was not ready to answer.

Twenty

"We're going to help build the housing part of the castle today, but I'm going to show you the room of dreams first," Barabus said as they walked through the forest again. He headed down a different path and soon the castle appeared before them, or at least the start of one. It rose high and was made of light grey stones. There was a drawbridge and a door at the front, with two towers on either side. As they walked through the gates, there was a centre courtyard area and beyond it was the main entrance into the castle.

"It's still a work in progress," Barabus said, motioning to the back of the castle. One tunnel left the back of the structure and ended in an open space. "We'll be adding to that when we can. It will be the housing section."

They entered through the main door and into a hall that had off-shoots to other halls and rooms. This was the more complete area of the castle, and soon she lost all sense of which way they were going.

He halted in front of a door that stood out from the others. It was a large, dark oak door with brass trim pieces and hinges.

Sarith had thought about this room all night. Every time she was about to drift off to sleep, another idea had come to her mind. She wasn't sure what it would be, but she had some ideas. It definitely had to have something to do with dreams, but what they did with them or how they worked, she couldn't even venture a guess.

He slowly pushed it open and stepped back so she could see inside. She walked in and stopped. The room had many long tables with tablecloths on them and old-fashioned typewriters on it. There were stacks of papers at the end of the tables and at the far right of the room was a table with four large wooden boxes on it.

Barabus walked around to the other side of the table and stopped in front of her. "Here is the room of dreams. This is where we write dreams for humans. It doesn't matter if it's the ones you have at night or during the day, we write them. Further into the castle, there is a room that gives us data sheets on each human. We take the information and we compile it. Once they are typed on the enchanted paper, then the human has that dream. Afterwards, the paper is transported to a storage room further into the castle, which we're still working on."

Sarith went to laugh at how absurd it all was, but the more she looked around, part of her felt like she could actually believe it. It all made sense and she could see how this was possible, especially since she had seen how she had a touch of magic.

"Maybe I could help?" she asked hesitantly.

"With the construction?"

"Well, yeah, that for sure… or maybe I could help here." Sarith said hesitantly.

"Absolutely not," a voice said behind them.

They turned, and Sarith was stunned to see Alex behind them. She hadn't heard him come in.

"Sorry, I didn't mean to step on any toes or anything."

"Helping with the town, or even the castle, would be fine, but not with this," Alex said. "Dream writing is for a select few. And there's the fact you are human that we have to consider too. I have a duty to protect this room. The answer is no."

His bluntness took Sarith back a step, but as she thought about it, she could understand where he was coming from. No one knew what would happen if she tried, but the idea of writing a dream and sending it to someone almost seemed too tempting to walk away from. She could send a dream to anyone. Everyone she knew dreamt, even if only a little. And what kind of dreams could she send? Her first thought was to send someone she loved a dream, telling them she's fine, but would they really believe it? Unless she actually went back home, there was no other way to contact anyone. And if she was truly honest with herself, going home was the least exciting idea she had had since getting here. She couldn't just yet.

The idea of writing a dream for a family member took hold. What harm could it do? It could just be to her daughter to tell her she was fine and didn't have to worry about her. It would only take a moment and no one would have to know about it.

Barabus looked back to Sarith, then to Alex. Alex fluffed up his wings and stood his ground.

"Why don't I show you around a bit more, and we'll make our way over to where James will live? We'll see how the building is coming along," Barabus said.

They walked out the door and Sarith saw Alex close it behind them.

* * *

"Come with me," Barabus said, heading down a different hallway.

"What's this?" Sarith asked, as they stopped outside a large wooden door with heavy iron hinges and a large handle.

"This is the mailroom," Barabus grinned at her, pushing it open, then moving aside so she could see the room.

In front of them was a long counter spanning the entire front of the room. Behind the counter, the walls on both the left and right sides displayed golden tubes that rose to the ceiling and vanished from sight.

Animals were pulling cylinders out from the ones on the left and putting the paper into wooden boxes that they moved to the front of the room. On the right, she watched as others were taking paper out of the boxes and were instead putting the paper into cylinders that they were sending up.

She was breathless from the beauty. Never had she seen anything like this before.

"The dream data sheets come in on the one side there, that help us write the dreams. They tell us all about the people and what they would identify with in their dreams for that night. The other ones take the written dreams away. Where, we don't know. No one has ever really known."

"So, you have to have those sheets to write the dreams then?" Sarith asked, trying to wrap her mind around the whole thing.

"Yep. If there isn't a data sheet, we can't write it."

"That's so cool."

"There are folks here that this is their only job. They deliver data sheets and take them away. It's a big job, but it has to be done."

They stood watching for a bit, and each animal worked together to get the dreams where they needed to go.

"That's amazing," Sarith whispered in awe.

"We should get going. People are likely waiting for us."

Barabus took her arm and pulled her to the door. She would have happily stayed here for hours if she could. This world was so much more than it had appeared at first. What else was here that she didn't know about?

Twenty-One

Barabus and Sarith exited the castle and walked toward the east wing. Things were coming along, but one hallway just ended into open space.

"What's going down at that end?" Sarith asked, pointing to the hallway.

"That's going to be bedrooms. In this case, James's rooms. He will be the one in charge of the dream-writing rooms. It makes it easier to be on hand, in case anything comes up."

Sarith turned to see a group of animals coming her way.

"James! I wondered if you'd come out here and give us a hand," Barabus said. James came over and shook paws with Barabus.

"Well, I know it's important I'm here for this," James said, sounding completely disinterested.

"We are going to be making a kitchen, bathroom, and a bedroom, or did you want two?" Barabus asked.

"Might as well make two," James said.

James walked over to a spot with thick clay and she watched as he added water and the two elements mixed and became a thick substance that he rolled in his paws.

Barabus was moving rocks and boulders into place like he had been with the town. Each stone lifted in the air and came down on top of the next, slowly building a wall. He paused after a row and James came over, pressing the clay into all the cracks and openings, sealing them tight.

The work continued like that for a while. Sarith kept her distance, but eventually she moved over to the next area and focused on each rock. The first one lifted into the air, and she pictured it moving over to the wall. It jutted this way and that, before finally making a shaky landing on the ground. It shook the ground, just enough that James looked over at her.

She returned his look, but went over to the next rock. She moved one rock at a time and, although it was a struggle, each one became easier and landed where it was supposed to.

Soon, she was ready for mud.

"What?" she asked as he came over and stood beside her.

"You're obviously getting the hang of it," James said, taking the clay he still had in his hands and headed over to the wall. He added it between the rocks before returning to her side.

"Yeah, I think so," she said, lifting the next rock. It came up and shook, before landing beside the wall. "I guess it's still a work-in-process, though."

James walked over to the rock and held his paws out to it. He seemed confused as she watched.

"That's strange. Why won't that lift?" James asked.

"That happened earlier in town. A few of the other animals tried to move a rock that I accidentally slammed into the ground and they couldn't. Let me try."

She reached out her hands to it and waited. A few moments went by before she finally saw it shaking, just slightly and without warning, it flung up into the air.

"Whoa!" James said, trying to see it up in the sky, but the sun blocked his view.

The rock went over their heads, town ward, before she yanked it back, causing it to sway above.

The rock hurled down and smashed into the wall she had been creating, destroying a large section near the end. The impact split the flung rock in two, leaving it open like an exposed wound.

"Well, crap," she said, eyeing the mess in front of her.

James reached out his paws and tried to move the rocks to fix what had been done, but nothing seemed to work. Sarith watched for only a moment before she reached out her hands and joined his efforts.

The rocks twitched and between the two of them, they managed to get the wall back in place.

"We'll have to get rid of that split rock," James said, inspecting the one on the ground by the wall.

"Can't we just... fix it? Like seal it back up?" Sarith asked.

"It would still have a crack in it, making it too weak," James said, thinking of his father's tombstone.

"Well, I could try," Sarith said.

* * *

James stood back as she reached over and touched one half of the stone. It rose up and turned. The broken edge came back down onto its matching half and stopped.

She put her hand on it again and closed her eyes. At first it didn't appear like anything was happening and James smirked to himself. He knew she wouldn't be able to do anything. But just as he was about to give up, he saw something that made his blood run cold. There, in the middle of the rock, he saw the seam of it slowly closing up, until the whole thing was one piece again. Not even a seam remained.

"What the—?" he managed.

"I did it?" she laughed. "This is the first thing that's actually gone the way I wanted!"

James walked around and let his paw run across where the seam had been. There wasn't even a mark to show it had been broken to begin with. How could someone so new to this world manage that when he couldn't even do it? James felt his blood boil as he looked to see if anyone else had seen it. Barabus was around the corner working on a completely different wall, unaware of what had just happened. This stupid rock, that meant nothing, was fixed, but somehow the tombstone couldn't be.

Then it hit him. Maybe Sarith could fix it.

"Hey," he said. "You did pretty well on that rock."

"Yeah," she said, still inspecting it, clearly distracted.

"I've never seen that before. Maybe you could help me with another rock I have that needs fixing."

"Oh yeah?" she asked, barely acknowledging him. She had her hands out now and was trying to move it. It rose with a shakiness again, but soon she had it up in the air and was carefully moving it to the wall. It came down with a loud thud, sending a vibration through the ground.

"This is incredible," she said. "I wonder what else I can do."

"Maybe you could fix another stone I know that's cracked?" James said, trying to get her attention.

"Uh yeah, sure, whatever," she replied, walking towards the pile of rocks.

Sarith went back to work and moved more stones. James could see that even though he was here, in her world right now, he wasn't. She was busy thinking about what else she could do with her magic and nothing was going to distract her.

"Sarith, maybe I can help you with your magic," he said, walking directly in front of her.

She finally met his eye-line and stopped what she was doing.

"Oh?"

"Yes. What if I give you some pointers and show you how we do some things with magic?" James asked.

"I guess that would be fine."

"Ok, well..." James started before Barabus interrupted them.

"Hey," he said, eyeing them both. "Can you help me with..." Barabus led Sarith away, but not before James gave her a look that made it clear that their conversation was far from finished.

114

Twenty-Two

Barabus spent the rest of the day helping Sarith as they worked on the walls of the castle. Every stone she moved became easier, and she felt like she was finally getting the hang of it. With the secondary bedroom, they tried to make furniture, but the one thing that had been so easy at home with her tools was nothing but a headache here in this world. Each piece she made came out strange and crooked. It made her blood boil, but she hoped that with time she could figure it out.

As the day drew to a close, Barabus went and talked to one of the others, leaving her on her own. James appeared out of nowhere and asked her to come by his place the next day. Barabus had some town business to attend to so she was free to do as she wished.

He had given her directions and even though it took her longer than it should have, she finally found her way there. As she approached, it wasn't quite what she had expected. She thought it would be bigger. But it was the gardens that really took her breath away. They were full of every kind of flower she could even think of and more. Some flowers she didn't even recognize and maybe it was just the sunlight, but she almost thought some were glowing. The gardens started at the front of the house and sneaked their way around to the backyard. She approached the front door and was about to knock when James cracked the door open a hair and slid out. Sarith heard something clatter beyond, but James immediately shut it and turned to her.

"Everything ok in there?" she asked.

"Oh yeah," he said, turning the key in the lock. She heard another rustle of something but when James walked away, she paused only briefly to look at the door again, before following him.

"So, I know Barabus has been showing you some magic," James began, "but each one of us here has a different magic. I'm hoping I can show you a few things that maybe he hasn't been able to."

"What kind of magic do you have?" she asked, jogging to keep up with his pace.

"I, well, I can do a few things, but I excel at gardening," he said, nodding towards the gardens she had just been admiring. Sarith readily agreed. She thought back to her own gardens at home and remembered how terrible they were. But even the thoughts of those gardens were getting fuzzy. Was it last year or this year that she had planted the things? What was it she had planted? Why did it all feel like a different lifetime ago?

"Although, I think my talents are shifting," James said.

* * *

Gardening, James thought. The word had meant so much to him over the years, but things definitely were changing. He said it with a tinge of pain as he thought about the tree he had tried to plant at his dad's gravestone. He hadn't dared touch the gardens here in case the same thing happened. Seeing them possibly turn to ash was more than he could bare.

"And the supervising," Sarith said.

She was right, of course, but just the thought of it made his blood boil. He heard a thud as the creature inside his house hit something and he forced himself to take another breath.

Calm. He needed to stay calm.

"I thought maybe we could try some gardening magic. I know that's not Barabus's gift, but it being mine, I think I can help."

James motioned for her to follow him and they went around back. Her mouth flew open in surprised awe. He lead her behind the gazebo to the corner of the yard that still needed to be filled.

He started explaining, similar to how Barabus had, how the magic works. She tried and tried, but as the day went on, he could feel his frustration rising. He was losing his patience, which he knew wasn't ok.

"You just have to think about what you're doing," he snipped at her.

"I am! I'm thinking about it. I'm trying!"

"Are you though?" He yelled, rolling his eyes. "It doesn't seem like it. I really need you to help me here."

* * *

Sarith stared at him and could almost see Luke's face reflected to her. The yelling and the eye rolling was exactly what he did. That was his way of trying to control the situation. And to control her response. It always made her feel like her thoughts and opinions weren't good or ok. That simple thing that most would think nothing of sent her brain into a spiral. She would not put up with this again. Not here. Not ever.

Without another word, she calmly turned on her heel to walk away.

"Where are you going?"

"I'm leaving."

James ran over to her and stepped in front of her.

"You can't leave. Please. I'm sorry. I didn't mean to get mad at you, it's just that I really want to help."

Sarith pushed past him and kept walking. She didn't care what he had to say. She was done with this nonsense.

"Listen, I'm sorry. I won't act like that again. I just, I know you can do this. I've seen what you did with the stone before. I really want…"

"I don't really care what you want."

"It's a gravestone," he said, calling back to her.

Sarith turned. She could see the hurt in there, but her heart felt hard. She had been yelled at and eye-rolled too many times to care anymore.

"My father's. There's a crack in the stone and I can't fix it." James said, his head drooping down.

"Well, I'm sorry you can't fix it on your own, but you should have thought about that before you reacted the way you did. If it's so important, you fix it."

"But I can't."

"I don't care." Sarith walked away and didn't look back. She didn't need to, to know that James was not following her.

Twenty-Three

Sarith walked toward the castle. She didn't know where Barabus was today, but she knew where she wanted to be. When she reached the end they had been working on yesterday, not much more had changed. The spare room James had requested was built, but not furnished. She'd start there. With her construction background, surely building things here wouldn't be that hard.

She spent the next few hours repeatedly trying to make the furniture. No matter how many times she tried, the pieces came out wonky. She couldn't get the joints to work properly, nothing was level, and the cut edges were all over the place. The day before, she had at least been able to make the building. Maybe she should try that again.

Walking outside, she held her hands up and watched as the stones nearby slowly, one at a time, came up and over towards her. She carefully put one down on top of the other until she had a wall. It was a small section and it already was off balance, but she kept going. She knew she had to get something done. She had to prove to herself and those around her she could do it.

As she worked, something James had said before came to mind. He couldn't fix the gravestone. After spending the last few days here, she had seen those around her doing so much and couldn't imagine them not being able to do something. But he had asked her for help because he couldn't. And now that she thought of it, he hadn't touched the gardens either. She was the one that did all the work. Something about it didn't seem right.

Once the wall was done, she finished a second one. It was wonky too. Sarith was sure they would fix it, but she was trying. She thought about that first rock she had flung into the ground. She hadn't meant to, but she had. It took an entire team to fix it. Would that mean that any of the wonkiness of her walls would take multiple animals? And why did it take an entire team, when other animals could make a mistake, and it only took one of them to fix it?

Maybe there was something different about her magic. Maybe what she did was stronger? Was this why James had asked her to come over and help him? He almost believed it, too. If her magic was stronger, then what did that mean for her and for them?

For the rest of the day, she spent her time working away, only stopping occasionally to rest.

As the sun started to set, she went back inside and let herself fall backwards onto the bed that Barabus had made the day before and sighed. She was exhausted. All she wanted was a bath, and a home cooked meal. That's one thing she hadn't tried yet was making food.

Maybe she would make something tonight for Barabus. He had done so much for her.

She sat up and walked to the door, putting her hand on the doorknob, when she heard voices outside in the hall. She opened the door a crack and, to her surprise, it was Alex, James, and Terrance.

"I'm concerned," James said. "I've seen her power and I'm worried that she's trying to do too much too soon."

"She's only been building. Barabus is keeping a close eye, and you watched her today. Where did you say she is now?" Terrance asked.

James paced in a circle. "She said she was heading back to Barabus's house. I would have gone with her, but I wanted to check in here."

"This isn't good. She wants to try writing a dream. There is no way that having a human try to write a dream for another human will end well. It's never been done before," Alex said.

"I understand, but she has done nothing wrong. All she has done is be kind and helpful."

"But did you see how it took a whole team to fix any of her mistakes over the last few days? There's something about her using magic that seems to be, I don't know, stronger." James said.

"I've noticed that too," Terrance said, rustling his mane. "But as long as she's not hurting anyone, we can't do much right now. We need to send a team down to the lake. Barabus thought she might have come through there. If we send some of the deeper swimming fish down to the bottom, maybe they can locate what's down there.

"Until we have more information, though, we just need to stay the course that we've been doing and we wait. We only act if needed, because if you are right, and she is stronger, then we need to have a plan to deal with it. It'll probably take the whole town to come against her, but we won't be able to otherwise."

"Ok," James said.

Even at a distance, she could hear the concern etched in them. It made her mad. She hadn't done anything yet. She hadn't even breathed wrong and here they were, being scared of her. It didn't seem right.

The trio in the hall walked away. She slipped out of the room and followed at a distance, trying to keep as quiet as possible. At the next hall, she darted down it and exited at the end to outside. The day was getting long and she wanted to get back to Barabus's house before he made anything to eat.

She was going to make him a dinner that would blow his socks off.

* * *

Sarith collapsed into bed and almost immediately felt sleep drifting over her. She was so thankful for the warm bed and the chance to rest. She wanted nothing more than to just lose herself in a good dream, but she wasn't even sure if that was possible. Since being here, she hadn't dreamt at all. That's one thing she missed.

The dinner for Barabus had gone better than she expected, but she still wished she had done more. It was a simple stir-fry, but she had used magic to cook it and it wasn't completely burnt. He had told her it was good, but she felt like maybe he was just trying to help her feel better.

She listened as Barabus moved around and although she enjoyed having someone to live with, she was finding she wanted some of her own personal space. Tomorrow she would find somewhere that was her own. And as the world around her faded away into sleep, she knew exactly where she would go.

Twenty-Four

The days melded together and felt oddly overwhelming to James. Every morning, he would meet Alex at the castle and they would go over the dream-writing room to learn more of the job.

James knew it was going to be a lot, but each day the weight of the responsibility became more and more crushing to the point of feeling like he wouldn't survive.

The job was more than just making sure they wrote the dreams. He also provided support to those needing it, then got the typed dreams into the enchanted boxes to be stored away. Thankfully, he could trust those around him to store the dreams in the proper place, but all the other tasks were becoming a lot. He knew that dream-writing was considered to be the most important and sought-after than any other job out there, but he didn't want it. It was the life that was chosen for him. It was the life he didn't have any say over. It was the life he would be stuck with forever.

His passion was growing plants, making things thrive and grow, but he didn't get to do that after all. He was stuck doing what he was told to do. Since being pushed into this whole thing, he had countless times to make plants grow, but nothing worked. He was always met with ash and dust. The anger and frustration from it all made him furious. The world was against him and he couldn't see a way out.

Worn thin, James made his way home, slugging through the woods to his house. He stopped multiple times, making sure no one was following him. James took one last look around before pulling the key out of his bag. He unlocked his front door and slipped inside. The door had three deadbolts and a handle lock. He turned them all, making sure it was secure, then he spun to face the room. Even from here, he could hear that creature moving around and scurrying in the distance. It was scratching against the door. If the creature kept doing that, he would have to replace the door again. It was the second one in two days.

He went to the side table in his living room, slid open the drawer, and pulled out a key. Going to the spare bed-room, he took a breath before putting the key in the lock and turning the knob.

The door pushed open the moment the lock was turned and the creature he had taken in only a short time ago ran past him, shoving him into the wall. It darted into the living room and knocked into a table. The lamp rattled and, for a moment, hung suspended in the air. James spun just as it was falling and held out his paw. A burst of light radiated out of it and stopped the lamp from hitting the floor. It pushed the lamp back onto the table and disappeared. Today, he didn't even need to measure to know this creature had grown again. He looked back at the spare room and saw that tables were knocked over and one bedpost had been chewed through and sat like a discarded chew toy on the floor.

The creature had settled down finally, and James stood up. His side hurt where he had hit the wall. He rubbed it and then went to the living room. The creature had thrown around things, but this time it didn't have time to break anything.

James finally got a good look at the creature. The thing was at least three inches taller than it had been the day before. Its hair was getting long and was sweeping the floor with each step. Its teeth grew sharp and one was longer than the rest. It wasn't as cute as it had once been.

His outburst and rising anger against Sarith had been hard to manage, and he could tell it was affecting this thing. But even then, he had been this angry before and it hadn't grown that much. Sarith had been burning with anger after their day working together. He could see it even though she had tried to keep herself calm. Clearly, he had set her off. He thought it was only his anger that made it grow, but after tonight, he wasn't so sure.

He pointed to the cupboard across the room, and the door flung open. A bowl and a bag of food came out and poured itself. It floated over to the creature and it ate hungrily.

"What am I going to do with you?" he asked the creature. For now, he could care for it, but as the pain still shot up his side, he knew he wouldn't be able to for much longer. This thing was getting too strong. He would have to find some way to either get help or pawn it off on someone. Only, no one he knew was strong enough to handle it. He barely could himself.

But then there was Sarith. Clearly, her magic was stronger if it took a whole team to undo her mess-ups. She had done things that none of the other animals had ever done. It scared and delighted him. Even though it wasn't perfect yet, it still needed some work. It was getting stronger by the moment. So strong, in fact, that she could manage this thing.

What a perfect idea, he thought. The next time Sarith had a major outburst again, he would plant this thing and convince her it belonged to her. And if he did it just right, he would pull it off.

Now it was just a matter of timing.

Twenty-Five

Sarith had been eyeing the one plot of land since the first day she had been shown the castle. It was nestled between two towering oak trees and was surrounded at the back by brush making it feel cozy. There was a freshwater creek flowing behind it, providing a continuous source of water. She wondered if it was an offshoot from the lake. There was something about being here that just felt so right. Trying to think back to her home, her family, it all felt like such a strange dream from years ago. The longer she was here, the hazier the lines of reality were getting.

This past week, she had been shadowing Barabus. Every time he built something, or helped around the town, she was there following along. But her magic was still coming out wonky. Just yesterday she had planned to make a garden of wild flowers and shrubs, but each time she tried, the plants either came out dead or burnt. A couple of them came out green, but they quickly overgrew and ended up ten feet tall.

The last few days, Cynthia had been teaching Woodrow how to use magic, and he figured out he had the gift of nature. He could grow almost anything he had set his mind to. She had him come over and help get the gardens in shape, but even he struggled to correct her magic. It ended up taking three of them to just make it happen.

With each passing day, she was determined to show she belonged here. The idea of going home, her real home, made her stomach turn. At some point, it had felt like she had waited too long to go back. Now it would almost be harder because it had been so long.

Sarith eyed the land in front of her and could see the idea of a house forming in her head. It didn't have to be big and, if she was honest with herself, she didn't think she'd have enough magic to make it very big. The house she pictured was simple and similar to the other homes in town. One big room with a kitchen, dining area, and a living area, while a bedroom shot off one end and a bathroom nearby. It wasn't anything like her home back in the real world, and that made it even more appealing.

Sarith extended her hands and took her stance. She closed her eyes and let the energy build before letting it release out her fingertips. Opening them again, she saw sparky purple bolts of lightning came out of her fingertips and shot over to the open area. Dirt came up from the ground in lines towards the sky. It took a moment, but she brought it back down and waited as it became compacted, forming thick walls. She reached her hand out to the left, where a small mound of dirt was, and brought it over slowly. It fell out of her reach a few times, crashing to the earth and making her hands and body tremble from the impact, but she brought it back up and motioned with her hands for it to smooth out above the walls to make the roof.

It came out rippled and lumpy, but she didn't care. She was finally creating something, and it was halfway working.

Sarith let her hands fall. Now she needed to do some work on the inside. She walked in and quickly got to work making a bed, a dresser, a bathroom, a full kitchen, all of which wasn't perfect, but she didn't mind. One side of the bed was longer than the other, the cabinets weren't totally square, and even the windows she put in weren't the same size, but it was hers and that's all that mattered. It was a place she could call her own and was enough.

As she was working, she heard someone come in the door and stop.

"Just a minute," she said as she finished creating a stove, the door of which didn't want to stay closed. She would have to fix that later. She turned and saw James standing inside her doorway, watching her work.

"What can I do for you?" she asked, shoving the stove door again. It came down with a crash. She let out a low growl under her breath.

"I was just wondering how things are going?" he asked.

She could see how he was doing a scan of the area, trying to make it look subtle, but he was terrible at it.

"They are coming along just fine," she said, but knew she really didn't believe it. "If there's nothing else, I really should get back to work."

James walked over to the stove and with a flick of his wrist, the stove door righted itself and he faced her again. Even from a distance, she could see the smug look on his face and she didn't like it.

"I don't need the help. I've got this under control, but thanks for stopping by," she said, walking over to the door and holding it open for him.

"Are you sure you do?" James said, walking to the kitchen table. He leaned on and it wobbled from uneven table legs. She watched as the table leg grew under the weight he was putting on the table and even itself out.

"Yes, I do." She nodded toward the doorway, wanting him to leave. Instead, he walked over to the couch she had tried to make that was at a weird angle and touched the bottom leg. Slowly, it righted itself and James took a seat.

"I know we got off on the wrong foot, but you want to stay here and I also know there are others that don't agree."

"Oh, is that so?" Sarith said, finally letting the door go. She stood with his arms crossed and waited.

"Yes. Maybe I can help you at least hone your magic enough that they will think about letting you stay instead."

Sarith sat down on the chair across from him and glared.

"Up to you. It's fine if you want to go home," James said.

Sarith knew he was baiting her. He must have something up his sleeve, but part of her didn't care. She wanted to stay and if it meant going along with whatever he was thinking, it might be worth thinking about.

"There are many here that don't think you do. They think you should head back home, wherever that is." James walked over to the kitchen sink that wouldn't stop dripping and with a twist of something underneath, it stopped.

"Well, I'm not going anywhere. I belong here just as much as anyone else."

James tilted his head towards her. "If you say so," he shrugged.

"I do!" she exclaimed. "I can make this magic thing work. I know you don't believe me, but I'll show you. I'm… I'm going to host a dinner," she stammered. "A dinner party. I'll invite everyone in town, and I'll show you. It'll be unlike anything anyone has ever seen before."

"And when should we expect this dinner to happen?"

"Three days from now."

"Sounds lovely," James said, sneering.

"I'll give you a list of names. Spread the word."

Sarith watched as James walked out the door and toward town. Her blood was pumping. But as it slowed, one thing rang in her head: What had she just gotten herself into?

Twenty-Six

It didn't take long for the word to spread about the dinner party. James told the ones that were invited, but it was once the town gossip heard that everyone knew and the town was buzzing with excitement.

He had taken some extra time getting ready, and he was running late. Walking up to her house, James saw Woodrow and a few others were already there. The air was electric. They were talking amongst themselves, holding glasses of bubbling drinks with pieces of fruit in them.

"Are we eating out here?" James asked, as a tray with glasses floated over to him. Cynthia laughed and shook her head.

"No, just cocktails. Sarith said something about needing to finish up a couple of last-minute details," she said, taking a sip of her drink.

"How has Woodrow been doing?" James asked Cynthia as he took a sip of his bubbly drink.

As if having heard his name, Woodrow bounced over and stood beside them.

"I'm doing great! Cynthia has taught me so much. Did you know that I have the gift of gardening? It's amazing to see the plants grow and flourish. I don't know if there's anything better than that."

James felt the heat rising in him again. He knew gardening was the best thing ever and it had been robbed of him, forcing him into a job he didn't want.

"Nothing better," James said with a pasted-on smile.

"She's told me you are a supervisor! That's quite the honour. You must love it."

"It is an honour." He didn't know if his words truly showed he believed it, but he turned his head and looked over the crowd. Not a single person was missing from the list she had given him. Everyone was so happy to be there, and the surrounding conversations buzzed.

"Has anyone seen Sarith since she announced the dinner?" James asked.

"Nope, no one," Cynthia replied. "I heard she locked herself in her house, working on everything. Terrance told me he walked by here yesterday morning and could hear her banging and clanging things. And then Alex told me he was flying home last night and saw the light pouring out over the yard from her place. She was working late into the night. I wonder what she has in store for us."

"I guess we'll find out soon," James said, draining his glass and looking for a tray to put it back on. One floated by and he set it down as a million fireflies gently floated their way up into the air and swirled around them. Cynthia laughed, while others oh'd and awe'd.

"Welcome everyone," Sarith said from behind them. They all turned and carefully clapped while holding their glasses. "I've been working on something extra special for tonight. I hope you'll like it."

She stepped aside, making room for them to enter her home.

She had set up the dining room with a long wooden table in the middle. Down the centre of it were sprigs of evergreens and candlesticks that lit the room with a warm aura. The table had ten seats on each side and one at the end, each with name cards for the guests. The spot at the head of the table remained empty for Sarith. James walked along it and found his seat was next to Sarith. Even he had to admit, this was all pretty impressive.

Candlelight lanterns were tucked in the corners of the room, while others hung from the ceiling and some floated by the walls. Once everyone sat, the talking stayed to a dull murmur until Sarith walked in. She was in a different gown than a moment ago. This one was a deep crimson red with black trim. It flowed to the floor and swept around her feet as she moved, making it look like she was gliding. Her long black hair was now tied in a loose bun at the back and ringlets framed her face. Even from her walk, James could tell she was excited about the night ahead.

* * *

Sarith locked eyes with James briefly, easily reading his doubting eyes. She wouldn't let James's doubt upset her.

Not tonight. Tonight, she was going to enjoy herself. She pulled her shoulders back and took a deep breath.

Turning to her guests, she beamed and let her eyes radiate the determination she now felt. She snapped her fingers and plates came floating from the kitchen. One by one, they floated into the dining hall and gently landed in front of each guest. Some laughed, while others squealed in delight as they saw the meal. There was a mixed green salad with dressing and topped with fruit and nuts.

They looked up at her expectantly, and she gave them a nod as she sat at the head of the table. A plate came to her, and she picked up her fork. Everyone was talking again, enjoying each bite, and she took one herself. Here, the fruit tasted so much sweeter and juicier than at home. She stopped. Home. She hadn't let herself think of home for a while now. She shook the thought off and watched her guests enjoy themselves.

James leaned over to her and whispered to her, "This looks nice. So far, so good."

Sarith smiled smugly at him. If tonight went as well as she expected, then she would show him and everyone else that she could handle this, and this was her home now.

As the guests finished up their fresh salads, Sarith raised her hand, and the plates lifted off the table and stacked gently on top of each other before floating out of the room and disappearing out of sight.

Delight spread across their faces, and Sarith finally felt like she could relax. Any fear that they may have had at one point was clearly gone. They were believing in her.

The next set of plates came out and on it were stuffed peppers, filled with chopped cauliflower, freshly made tomato sauce, green beans and mushrooms, then topped with melted cheese.

The plates set down and everyone dove in. Conversation was lively and Sarith even let herself finally talk to some of her guests. No one talked about her use of magic and she had to admit, she was glad of it. As they finished up and before dessert was about to come out, Sarith stood with her wineglass in hand.

"I want to thank everyone for coming. I know some of you had some reservations about this, but I appreciate you giving me a chance to show you I am capable of doing some magic.

"When I first arrived, you all were understandably nervous, but you let me see your world and stay here even when you didn't always know what was going to happen. You accepted me and for that I will always be grateful. I feel at home." Sarith beamed at the table, which returned her smiles and she raised her glass. "To us."

They all took a drink. She took one too but remained standing.

"I have one more thing for us before dessert comes out."

As her magic increased, she knew some of them were getting nervous, but this would be the time to show them all. They would finally understand.

She held out her hands towards the ceiling, and everyone in the room turned.

* * *

James looked up, wondering what she could possibly be meaning to do with this. The roof vibrated. Above him, the ceiling opened up, then folded back on itself, revealing the star filled inky black night sky.

James's eyes flicked to Sarith, but she didn't take her eyes off what she was doing. Hands held out, he saw a swarm of fireflies come together and swirl in the sky. They started at the bottom of the opening and made loops until they left the view on the top right. A grin crept from Sarith's lips.

She snapped her fingers and in the distance, a tree branch came into view from somewhere nearby and a pair of giraffes were lowered from it, one on a ring and one on silks. They came right down to just above the roof and began an aerial act. The pair dipped and spun, while the guests gasping and softly clapping. They used their necks to hang off of the rings. Then shifted and suddenly their legs were out to their sides, making them appear weightless.

James watched as Sarith finally sat and nodded at the giraffes. He was sure she could sense his gaze, but she kept her eyes on the show. The rings and silks lowered, and the giraffes did a backflip off and landed beside the table. Fireworks erupted in the sky.

The dinner guests erupted in applause and got to their feet. She reached for her glass and stood. The night had gone perfectly. Even James wouldn't be able to dispute that. Now they would have to let her stay. The group cheered as she raised her glass. They all reached down and grabbed their glasses.

"Thank you all. Dessert will be out shortly, but for now, enjoy yourselves."

* * *

Sarith took a sip from her glass, and everyone followed suit. Everyone except James, of course. This time, it didn't bother her. Even he would have to admit everything had gone perfectly. She tried to wash the smug smile off her face, but she knew he could see it. There was something more under that look he was giving her. He almost seemed impressed.

"I'm not going to say it," he mumbled.

"You don't have to," she said, letting her eyes drift back to the sky above. The wind was shifting, and a chill filled the air. Overhead, the stars were disappearing as a wall of clouds rolled in. A thick raindrop fell down onto the plate in front of Sarith. Another fell onto James's head.

A few guests laughed, while others got up and ran over to the part of the room still covered.

"No problem. Let me just take care of this," Sarith said, standing up and raising her hands toward the ceiling again. The roof trembled, and James saw the two halves of it rising, but something didn't look right. The piece on the left was lifting too high. His eyes darted to her, and he could tell that she could see it.

"Do you—" he started, but stopped.

Concern washed over her face. She could feel all eyes on her, but she kept hers on what she was doing. Hands held up, she pulled down with her left hand, trying to pull that part of the roof back in line with the other one, but it wasn't working. Instead, the ceiling rose higher and higher. She pulled again, this time, putting all her body weight into it.

The roof shot down and collided with the right side, breaking it apart and sending pieces down towards them. Someone shrieked, and then there was chaos.

Everyone ran towards the door as chunks of rock came flying down to the table, crashing through the wood. A rainfall of dust showered over everything.

James ran to the door and held it open, shouting for everyone to get out. Sarith was trying to push the one side of the roof up again and over so it would come down properly but both sides were shaking back and forth. James could see beads of sweat forming on her brow. Once the last guest was gone, he ran over to her, looking back at the ceiling before pulling her hard. She tried to shake him off, but he grabbed her around the waist and pulled. She didn't take her eyes off the roof, and kept her hands towards it. They were the only thing keeping it from falling.

He got her to the door and only then did she let her hands fall. They stood in the doorway together and watched as the roof came crashing down, sending a tidal wave of dust and wood chunks flying. James and Sarith spun away and the pieces hit their backs as they ran out of the door and into the yard. The dust cloud blew over everyone before dispersing and leaving a thick layer of dust on everything.

Everyone started coughing and hitting the dust off themselves.

Sarith peered at James, and even through the dust and dirt, she could see the disapproval in his eyes. She could see what he was thinking even before he said anything.

"I couldn't know this was going to happen," she said, trying to stop him from saying what she knew he wanted to.

"Don't you say it," Sarith said, pointing to Alex as he walked over and then to James.

"It's something we need to talk about," Alex said.

"No we don't. I made one mistake. One! The dinner was going fine until then. And it only got messed up because of you," she said, pointing to James again.

"I didn't do anything."

"You didn't? What about the look you gave me? I knew you were judging everything. You aren't exactly subtle with your expressions."

"I did nothing," he said shortly.

"Listen, maybe you should think about taking a bit of a break with the magic for a bit, or at the very least, don't be doing anything as big as all this. Maybe you are just… doing more than you should." Terrance said, as he joined them. She knew he was trying to be gentle and calm about it, but she was mad.

"What do you know about how much I should do? You know nothing of what I'm capable of!" she yelled.

"What you are doing is so far beyond what we've ever done here before. Maybe our world isn't meant to do all this."

"So, am I supposed to just stop using magic?"

Alex looked at James, who looked back at him.

"What was that?"

"There are those wondering if your magic is too much for our world," James said, finally meeting her eyes again. Behind them, James could see the fire burning as the words settled in her and she understood what he was implying.

"I have just as much right to be here and do this as any of you," she said, glancing around at the guests that were now quietly listening to the argument.

She looked at their faces; a few looked down to the ground, avoiding eye contact. They didn't have to say the words for her to know they wanted her to leave.

"We've been wondering for a while about whether or not what you've been doing is right for here... and we think it might be too dangerous for you to be doing this," Alex said.

"I'm doing just fine. This entire meal was fine until dessert. Don't I get even a little bit of credit for that?"

"If you're going to take credit for that, you better take it for almost crushing us to death," James spat at her.

Sarith scoffed and moved only inches away from his face.

"Leave. You're not welcome here," she hissed through clenched teeth.

"Fine. But as long as you know, neither are you." James spun and walked away. The others stood stunned, unsure of what to do now. Sarith looked at them and hesitated only for a moment before turning on her heel and walking back inside and slamming the door shut.

Twenty-Seven

The dinner party guests stood frozen in place as the door slammed shut behind them. There was a moment of silence before James and Alex turned to them.

"Well, that didn't go the way we expected," Alex said to James.

"No, I don't think so either," James said.

"So, what do we do now?" Alex asked.

"Drinks on me!" Woodrow said to the crowd.

"That's probably a good idea," James said as he followed.

Murmurs went through the group before they headed towards town.

* * *

They arrived in the tavern a short walk later. Someone was in the corner playing acoustic guitar, but the place was empty. The barkeeper saw them coming and immediately got out some glasses, setting them up for drinks. The other dinner guests filed in behind them and quickly filled the place.

James and Alex sat down at the bar as two beers slid down to them. Alex lifted his glass and waited for James to do the same.

"Well, here's to… quite the evening," Alex said, as he took a long drink.

"Yes, quite the evening indeed," James said, setting his glass down instead of taking a drink.

"What is it?" Alex asked, putting his down too.

James's eyes drifted around the room. He had grown up with these folks. They were the ones that had helped him when his mother died, then his father. They were the ones that had loved and respected his parents and his grandparents. And they were the ones that would follow his lead if he were to stand up against Sarith.

Most of them were laughing, almost like they forgot what had just happened. They were too calm. One of them picked up a violin and joined the guitarist, while another started singing. Cynthia walked past with a tray of drinks while swaying to the beat. She had clearly gotten past what had just happened.

"We've never seen anything like that before," James said to Alex. "I don't have a good feeling about this."

"I've been saying that since the start," Alex said, taking another drink.

"I think you were right," James said.

Woodrow came over and noticed James hadn't drunk anything yet. "Man, what's going on? We might have had a rough night, but it's all good now. Let's party like we had planned."

James smiled, but he felt unsettled. What would Sarith do now? And would she have another outburst? And if so, what would happen? Something was pulling at him. He couldn't just sit here and do nothing.

"Listen, I know she might have scared us, but it's fine. Things will be fine," Woodrow said, slapping his buddy on his back.

"Yeah," James said, pushing his drink over to Alex and standing.

"Where are you going?" Alex said, putting his hand around James's glass.

"I'm heading home. I'll see you guys later."

"But why?"

"I just, it's been a long night. Goodnight," James said as he left.

Twenty-Eight

Sarith took in the scene around her and what was her home. Everyone was long gone. She figured they had headed to town, probably to talk about how badly she had screwed up. Sarith could only take a couple of steps inside before she reached the rubble. The house was destroyed. She would have to rebuild. Heat rose in her cheeks, and she stomped her foot down so hard the ground shook. She jumped back as the mound that used to be the roof shifted and slid towards her. Sarith had worked on it for most of the week, trying to make it just right. She was determined to make her space everything she hadn't had before at her other home. The thought hit her hard: her other home. How long had she been in this world now? She wasn't even sure anymore.

Melissa. The name that rang in her head like a gong shaking her. She had left her; her early teen daughter, when she would have needed her the most.

The crushing weight of guilt washed over her. The joy and heartache tore at her heart. Now, she not only had her daughter and her family back home that were gone, but everything she had been trying to build here was too. No one would trust her again. And why would they? She had gone and screwed up this much.

But it hadn't been completely her fault though, had it? She had done everything she could to fit in with the animals here. She had learnt their ways and their magic, but nothing ever seemed to be enough for them.

Sarith raised her hands and held them out to the mound. The rocks trembled, but didn't move. Her hands were shaking, not out of fear, but anger. She let out a growl before spinning on her heel and walking out. She waved her hand towards the rubble. Like an explosion, the rocks went flying and landed hard on the earth, leaving deep craters. Sarith felt the trembling around her, but she didn't look back.

She wandered through the forest. Going to town was out of the question. She didn't want to face the townsfolk again. And after the other conversation she had overheard, she couldn't risk being seen near the lake in case they figured out that was how she came in and tried to force her to go home.

The darkness of the night gave her a bit of an advantage, as she was harder to spot, but she knew she couldn't wander all night. She would have to find somewhere to stay, whether she rebuilt or found somewhere that would let her in.

Lost in thought, she didn't notice she had arrived at the castle until the towers rose into view above the trees

To Sarith's surprise, the front gate was still unprotected, even after what happened tonight. Knowing how important those dream-writing rooms are, she assumed they would be the first thing protected. Good thing for her, though, they weren't yet.

Quietly, she slipped inside the front door and into the entryway. Immediately, she could hear the slapping of the keys as the animals wrote the dreams. Following the sound, she tiptoed down the dimly lit hall. She crept along the shadows, getting closer to the room.

The clock outside the dream-writing room read only ten o'clock. It would be hours before they were done, and she needed to get some sleep. They used most of the castle, but there was that section they had been working on before. She could easily stay there and no one would be the wiser.

The air was getting cold as she put more space between herself and the dream-writing room. A stiff wind passed over her as she rounded another corner. The incomplete hallways ended in just open sky and field. At least the room they had been working on the other day was closed in. She opened the door and was happy to see that while she was working on her own house, someone else had made furniture and finished the fireplace. It even looked like someone had tried it out with a couple of burnt logs.

It wasn't a big room, but it was comfortable. Already the bed had covers on it and there was a lamp on the bedside table. She snapped her fingers, and the fire started. Immediately, the warmth washed over her and she held out her hands. They were still shaking, but as the heat seeped into them, she felt herself calm down.

This is not how she had envisioned her night going. She was supposed to be admired by the town and going to sleep in her warm, cozy bed. Not in this place, a place she didn't even really know. As she got herself into this new bed, she pulled the covers up high. She hoped sleep would come quickly, but she wasn't banking on it.

* * *

Hours came and went, but sleep did not. Even at this distance, she could hear the clacking of typewriter keys. There was one animal that was particularly loud and she could tell anytime that one stopped typing to return pages because she would have a few moments where she almost fell asleep, but then they would start again and she would be startled out of her sleep. The cold air chilled her through the pile of blankets. Walking over to the fireplace, she put a few logs in it and found a match on the mantle. It struck quickly, and she threw the flame into the fireplace. It only took a few moments before the log caught and she felt the warmth creeping into her bones. She held her hands out. The clattering of the typewriters was still going, but the crackling of the fire was a welcome distraction.

Why hadn't she just used magic to make the fire? She suddenly thought as she looked down at her shaking hands. Everything about tonight felt off.

Soon she realized the noise around her was no longer as loud. The writing session was ending. She waited with bated breath for it to start again, but minutes dragged on and after a half hour, she knew they must have gone home.

She crept to the door and poked her head around the doorframe. Not a sound was to be heard as she slipped herself through the opening and tiptoed down the hall. She peaked around the corner and saw a light flick off. Slipping back out of sight, she waited. A door closed and Sarith carefully tilted her head as the last animal left the room, pulling the door closed behind him. The typists must have finished for the day. Another moment and his heavy steps faded as he walked the other way. She saw he had left and extinguished the lights on the way. He definitely wasn't coming back tonight.

Sarith walked up to the wooden door and gave it a push. It groaned slightly, but she wasn't worried about that. No one was around. The room was dark, but she knew there were wall sconces that could be light with a little magic. She held out her hands and watched as, one by one, the lights came to life and filled the room with a warm glow.

She didn't know what had led her here exactly, but seeing the typewriters, something awoke in her. The thought of her daughter came to her again. She wondered if someone had just recently written her a dream. Maybe even tonight. After being told she shouldn't try to write a dream, she had let it go, fearing they would make her leave this land. But after tonight, what did she have to lose? If the animals here could write dreams, why couldn't she?

Twenty-Nine

Sarith knew exactly which typewriter she wanted to use. The day she had been shown the dream-writing room, one had stood out to her. The one over in the corner had looked so different from the rest because it wasn't the typical black, brown, or other muted colours. This one was a soft sea-foam green with white keys. It reminded her of one piece of jewelry from the store. She shook off the thought and sat down. She let her fingers glide along the casing.

Sarith wiggled her fingers and took a deep breath. She was so excited she almost couldn't keep it together. She let herself touch the typewriter keys and a wave of emotions washed over her. This was really it. There was no one around to stop her. There was nothing left to lose.

She fed the thick paper through the machine and hit a key. It slapped up loudly. She took another deep breath and started.

Even though her daughter was only fourteen, she had found a love of mountain climbing. She had found a group in town that had let her join, even though she was still a bit too young.

Sarith didn't know much about it herself, but she tried to write about it the best she could. She used the nearby mountain as inspiration and wrote what she remembered of what it looked like, from the rocky face to the snowy peak that seemed to reach impossibly high. The sharp edges and cliffs would normally scare even some of the more seasoned hikers, but not her daughter. She would have looked that challenge up and down and then climbed it without hesitation. She was like her dad that way when they were younger. He never would have let anything stop him from doing what he put his mind to. Sarith had wished she was like that, but in reality, there was always something holding her back from the biggest adventures, and it was usually fear, or not feeling good enough.

Sarith stopped her fingers and shook the thoughts from her mind. She didn't want to think about her failures, or him. Especially him. She didn't want her dream for her daughter to be sullied.

She returned her thoughts to the mountain. She described it as best as she could and there, waiting at the top, was Sarith. Melissa reached the top and Sarith had a picnic lunch in hand.

She took her daughter by the hand and motioned for her to sit on the tablecloth she had put down.

"I don't have much time. Just know I'm sorry. I'm sorry for leaving you. I hope someday you will forgive me. I left because I couldn't do it anymore. Your dad isn't the guy you think he is. He wasn't the guy I thought he was, either. I didn't mean to direct my anger towards you. I know I was wrong. I hope you forgive me. Oh sweet girl, I'm so so sorry. I'm so sorry.

"I'm in a better place now. Wait, I shouldn't say it like that. I'm not dead, just free. I'm able to be the person I want to be and I'm hoping I will grow and someday become the person you need me to be. I love you, my dear sweet girl.

"Stay with your aunt. She knows how to take care of you better. Your dad doesn't know these things. You should be able..."

Sarith stopped. All around her hands, smoke rose from the typewriter and her hands. The paper started to smoke, while the bottom edge appeared to be melting and jamming up the casing. She jumped back and quickly looked around her. She grabbed one of the dust sheets and smacked the typewriter until the smouldering went out.

"What in the—" she said.

Maybe it was just the typewriter she was using.

She moved to the next one and tried to continue the dream, but the same thing happened. She did it again and again before she came to the typewriter at the end of the row and fell into the chair. Every time, the paper started to burn and jam the machine. All she had wanted to do was to send her daughter a message, but even that she couldn't get right.

Eyeing the typewriter in front of her, she could feel the heat rising in neck. She was so mad, she started pounding the keys. They snapped and went flying, but she didn't care. Her knuckles hit and blood gushed out, but she didn't stop. Over and over, she hit it. Blood now pounded into the keys and casing.

Sarith walked around the table to the other side of it and picked up a typewriter, ready to throw it across the room, but instead, she sat at it. She could feel the anger surging through her so deeply she couldn't stop herself. She thought about the anger her husband had shown towards her when she was fired from the jewelry store. Sarith knew he was banking on that being their way out of debt and being a part of the rich lifestyle he had so deeply craved. She thought he was different, but it didn't take long for her to see the truth. Only a few short months.

She stopped and rubbed her neck. Feeling the chain that had been around her neck since she arrived, she pulled it out of her dress and looked at it. The ruby stones were stunning. It didn't matter how many times she looked at it, she had always loved it. It made her laugh at how long it had taken Miles to notice it was missing. Her way of stealing it wasn't even clever. She had tucked it into her sleeve when she was closing up one night. Immediately she thought she'd be found out, but it took days before he asked, and he only did because he had sold the store, and couldn't find the payment for it.

But this place had finally made her feel like she wasn't just there to make money. The magic. The power. She had the chance to be and do whatever she wanted. She had a voice. And unlike at home, she wasn't afraid to use it.

Not afraid, she thought as she looked at the typewriter again. If anything, she was confident for the first time since she had gotten married. Her husband's face came to her mind and immediately anger burned in her again.

She hit the keys, only this time she let her fingers fly across them. Her anger fueled each word she wrote. And with each one, her anger grew. She could feel it coursing through her veins now, and she hit the keys harder and harder. Dark images filled her mind and she let all the unspoken anger course through her and out onto the page. She was done letting him and his anger make her feel small. She was done listening to his yells. She was done watching his eye rolls.

Sarith typed until finally she finished the dream, the dark, horrible dream, and she fell back exhausted, but the dream had given her a surge of energy she didn't have before. It was intoxicating, similar to an adrenaline rush, but somehow stronger. She closed her eyes and felt the throbbing in her fingertips. Looking down, she saw black ink seeped through her fingerprints. She wiped her hands on her pants, trying to clean them, but when she pulled them back up, the black ink was seeping out again, almost like she had just had her fingerprints taken at the police station.

She finally looked at the typewriter, the thing that had done that horrible deed, and she could see it. The paper was nearly filled, and it hung at a strange angle from the reel. She carefully nudged it and saw the paper was still intact. It hadn't started to smoke or melt like the others.

Was it her speed in typing? A dream of repentance to her daughter fell short, but the dream of anger somehow worked? She stood and stretched. Even after all the energy she had just put into writing, she somehow felt stronger than even before. She laughed. It felt good.

Leaning over, she ripped the paper out of the typewriter and glanced it over. She scoffed at it and let it fall to the floor. If he really got that nightmare, then maybe he would understand. She stomped on the paper and turned on her heel, making sure it was really driven into the dirt and walked out.

Thirty

James burst through the doors of the pub, the cold air hitting him and reviving him. He headed towards home. He had to check on the animal and collect his thoughts. The images of Sarith's ceiling would forever be etched into his memory. What would she do in this moment after everything that had happened? He wasn't sure, but he had a feeling he needed to act quick.

He walked through the forest in silence, unsure what he expected when he got home, but everything appeared the same from the outside. But that didn't feel right either. He put his paw on the doorknob, took a deep breath, and opened the door.

The house might have looked normal, but the inside was anything but. Tables and chairs were knocked over, lamps broken, and pieces of fabric, food, and papers were tossed everywhere. If he hadn't known better, he would have thought he was robbed. But he knew who the true culprit of this was.

His eyes scanned the place and asleep in front of the cold fireplace was the creature. James's breath caught in his throat. The animal now almost filled the room.

He quietly approached it, and it rolled toward him. Its tongue flopped out of its mouth. A few sniffs later, the animal awoke and blinked lazily for a moment. It jumped to its feet, bumping the ceiling. James had to take a step back before he could really take in the sight before him. The beast had changed in its features. No longer did it look like a sweet animal that could be his pet. Its eyes had changed and almost glowed. His fur was now rough and matted, deeper black than before. The odour coming off of him made James stop short. This morning he hadn't smelt like this, but tonight he emitted a stench that reminded him of rotting food. Now, he looked more like a beast.

It came over to James and nudged him for a pet, but it was so hard it sent him stumbling. James scurried back as quickly as he could and the animal sat, shaking the room and crushing a chair. James backed up, keeping his eyes on it, and slowly opened the door. The beast cocked its head to the side for a moment, then came bouncing toward him. He ducked just as the beast jumped and crashed through the doorway. The door flew outside, spinning end to end before landing with a thud. One corner sunk deep into the ground.

He ran out of his home. He would have to fix that, especially if anyone came looking for him. Or, maybe, just maybe, this was perfect. The folks in town would think Sarith attacked him. After the way things were left, they would think she was the one that caused the destruction.

But first, he had to find Sarith. She was likely at her house trying to rebuild, so he'd check there first.

He took a few steps outside the door, and the beast followed behind him.

It seemed every time he got angry, this thing grew. Tonight's events made it seem to grow even more, though, and he had remained composed. Sarith was the one that got angry tonight. It hit him. He wasn't the only one that could make it grow. And it made sense. She had more magic, stronger magic. Why wouldn't it affect everything around her? Including this.

The idea came to him like a lightning bolt. He could plant this thing at her destroyed house and convince the townsfolk it had to be hers. He knew they would believe him. Now, he just had to get it there without being seen.

* * *

James didn't need to check to know the beast was following him. The ground shook with every step.

In the distance, he could see the pile of rubble that was Sarith's home. Part of him wondered if Sarith had decided to leave this land after the terrible way the evening ended, but his gut told him otherwise. Even without seeing her, he knew she was around somewhere.

James walked up to the rubble and walked around it. He remembered how nice it had been when she finally finished making it. He actually had liked it and if he had had the chance to make his own place, he wondered if it would have been much different than what this house was.

The beast came up beside him, eyeing the pile in front of them and jumped on it. Soon he was trying to dig a hole into the stones and James watched as one by one it moved stones out of the way and burrowed itself down deep.

James tried to get it to come out, but the thing wouldn't move. It was almost as though it was too comfortable where it was. The beast had appeared after his outburst of anger, so he could say it was the same thing about why it was at Sarith's place, then it wouldn't be far from the truth. Lies are always more believable when they are close to the truth. James sat with the beast for a while until the thing fell asleep, its rhythmic breathing shifting to deep and long breaths.

He stood and tossed some food its way and walked away toward the castle. If Sarith wasn't at her house, he could think of nowhere else she could be other than the castle. And if he was right, that was only the start of their problems.

Thirty-One

The smell of hot paper reached James even before he reached the dream-writing room. He darted in and flicked on the lights. At the far side, he saw it. The typewriters were uncovered and a small trail of smoke rose from them.

He looked over the typewriters he used to love. They were now covered in something he didn't even recognize. He touched the very edge of it and read a couple of words. The paper smouldered and had melted into the typewriter and the keys stood at strange angles, no longer able to do its job. And it wasn't just one, it was machine after machine. He shook his head. He tried to make out any words on this melted mess of paper, but nothing came back clear.

Then he saw a single piece of paper crushed into the dirt. The words were at a crazy angle, but even through the footprint on it, they were still readable. The words told of something so bad, he quickly crumpled the paper up.

She had written a bad dream. Their world had never had bad dreams written like this before. It was only ever happy or nice dreams. Something like this was completely different, and it sent shivers down his spine. He didn't even know the typewriters were capable of this. Yet, here it was. Glancing at the paper, he flung it across the room. With the ruined paper inside, the typewriters were now useless. Grabbing one off the table, he then threw it to the ground, it smashing into millions of pieces. One after another, he pushed them off the table. He slammed his fist down and yelped as a shard of typewriter casing pierced it.

He watched as the blood drained down his paw and hung on for a moment before finally falling to the dirt at his feet. He kicked at the floor, hiding the drops, and went to leave.

Sarith was angry. If her anger could cause the paper to burn and melt, what else could it do?

He ran over and grabbed the dream he had crumpled and put it back on the floor where she had left it. He looked at the ones he had smashed and he knew he could easily say Sarith did it in a fit of anger. Sarith had lied to them already, so even if she denied it, they would assume she was lying. He just needed to get the others here and convince them of his story. It wouldn't take much. They trusted him. As far as they knew, he hadn't lied to them yet.

He walked out of the dream-writing room with a smirk on his face. It was all coming together now.

Thirty-Two

The pub felt warm to Alex, and he longed for the cool night air outside. Walking out, he was only there a few minutes before Woodrow and Terrance followed him.

"You ok?" Woodrow asked as they walked up behind Alex.

"Yeah, no. I don't know. I've got a weird feeling about everything this evening.

"James sounded like he was going home. I think we should go check on Sarith. She's had a rough night and who knows what she might do after this. If we can get her calm enough, we should try to convince her to head home. Having her here is dangerous. Something is bound to happen," Alex said.

"I wish she had finished telling us how she could get home," Terrance said.

"I know, but we can't dwell on that now. We need to get moving," Alex said, walking away.

* * *

Alex circled James's house overhead, but even at a distance, he could tell something was wrong. They landed beside the door, still stuck in the ground at a weird angle.

James's house was in shambles.

"James!" Woodrow called out, but was met with silence.

"Where is he?" Terrance said as he ran towards the back of the property.

Alex carefully approached the house and called out, but he could see it was abandoned.

"Where else would he have gone?" Woodrow asked, coming back to Alex.

"We need to check Sarith's house. I have a bad feeling about this," Alex said.

* * *

The trio went to what remained of Sarith's house. Woodrow knew if he had had to find this place on his own, he wouldn't have been able to. The pile of rubble seemed bigger than it had when they left earlier. There was no way that it had been that large before. Sarith's house was only a modest size when it was built, so seeing the size of the rubble almost seemed unreal.

The three of them slowed as they approached. Woodrow couldn't take his eyes off of it. It was like the ground was swelling and contracting. But then, that couldn't be right. Waves of heat came over him.

"Guys…" Woodrow started, but Alex held his arm out to stop Woodrow.

Terrance crept up to the mound and around to the side. He was only gone a few moments before he came back, and he looked whiter than a sheet.

"What is—" Woodrow started, but Terrance shook his head violently and held up his finger to shush him.

Terrance pointed the way they had come and mouthed one word that sent shivers up his spine, "Run."

Woodrow went to turn, but some movement from in front of him stopped him dead.

The large mound rose. With a fluttering of some fur, he was staring into the eyes of something huge. Another gust of heat washed over them as it breathed out and its eyes focused. Its mouth opened up, and razor-sharp teeth glared at them. A large pink tongue flopped out, and it was panting.

He had seen nothing like this before. Was it a bear, or a wolf, or even a dog? He didn't know, but sheer terror swept over him. His brain said run, but his legs wouldn't move.

Terrance reached over and grabbed his arm, yanking him to come as they ran. Woodrow tried to keep up with the other two as best as he could. All he wanted at this point was to be safe.

Thirty-Three

James barely left the castle when he heard a commotion in the distance.

"James?" He heard Alex say as three of them burst from the woods. "James! You're ok! We were worried." Alex flew over to him and put his large wings around him.

"Worried?" James asked, waiting for them to keep going. He needed to know what they knew first before saying anything further.

"We went to your house," Woodrow explained, "and saw what happened. Then we went to Sarith's house and found, well, I don't know what that thing is, but I'll never forget its razor-sharp teeth."

James saw the terror in their eyes. He knew they had seen the beast. He was just relieved they were ok.

"Where do you think that thing came from?" Terrance asked, trying to smooth out his fur.

"I don't know, but it was very comfortable at Sarith's. I have to imagine it was hers."

"Do you think it attacked James's house because she was mad at him for being so right about the dinner party?" one of them asked the group.

"My house is destroyed?" James asked, trying to sound like he didn't know.

"Oh James! You haven't seen it yet. It's a mess. It's not completely destroyed, but it's not good. Your place is in shambles," Woodrow said, his eyes glistening with tears.

"I thought you said you were going home?" Alex said, suddenly.

"I was, but uh, I realized if Sarith was going to do any-thing, it would be here at the castle," James said, looking at them both with as much sincerity as he could muster, hoping they would believe it.

"Good thinking. The dream-writing rooms are of the utmost importance. They need to be protected," Alex said. "Have you been inside?"

"I have. And you won't like what you see. We need to go get the others. They need to know what happened," James said.

Alex flew off. James, Woodrow, and Terrance headed inside the castle. They waited anxiously for everyone to come. Thankfully, they didn't have to wait long.

* * *

There was standing-room only as James held the type-writer up high in the air.

"Sarith tried to dream write." Everyone gasped when they saw the burnt, melted paper. He put it down and clutched the crumpled page with the typing on it.

"Here's what she was trying to write that burned, then melted the page," James said. "This page shows it. It gave me chills. I'll spare you the details, but it was the worst thing I had ever read in my life. It wasn't even a bad dream, it was worse. It was a nightmare."

An audible gasp filled the air, then the murmuring started. James nodded his head solemnly.

"We must confront her on this. She is now a threat to our way of life! If she doesn't go, who knows what else she'll be able to do! But we must go together. We will only succeed if we go as a united front," James said.

The townsfolk agreed, and Terrance came up beside him, gently putting his paw on James.

"I agree with James," Terrance said, scanning the crowd in front of him. "We need to talk to her and tell her she needs to go. She's getting too strong and is doing things that none of us have ever been able to do. The dinner party showed that. And now with this..." he said, letting his voice trail off.

"There's something else," Alex said, coming over as they all watched. "There is a beast at her house. It's larger than her house had been, and was too comfortable at her place to belong anywhere else!"

"This typewriter is damaged now," James said. "I don't know if we'll be able to fix it. We can't afford to lose any more typewriters."

The crowd was growing in volume, agreeing with them as they talked.

"I think we need to talk to her about this. We have to tell her how we feel," Terrance said above the voices.

"Where is she?" someone asked from the crowd.

"Right here," Sarith said, coming out from the room next door. "And I am not going anywhere."

* * *

Sarith had heard everything said, including this thing about the beast. She didn't understand what they were talking about, but if it was at her place, maybe it was hers.

"Listen—" Terrance started, but she let his words fade into the background. Concern was written all over their faces, but there was something deep etched in each one of their eyes. She saw something she hadn't seen before: fear. James was fidgeting with his paws; Woodrow looked around but avoided eye contact, and even Terrance's voice sounded less confident and in charge than it had before.

"We really think at this point that maybe you should consider heading home..." Terrance said, then paused. He stood with his large, full mane framing his face. She remembered the first time she had met him and the fear that had surged through her. Back at home, a lion would tear her apart, but here she was, staring at one that suddenly looked so small and who was definitely terrified of her.

Home.

That was the one word that came to her. None of them knew what home was like for her. If they did, they would never ask her to go there. They would figure out a way for her to stay.

"This has never happened before," Alex said. "And we can't afford for any more typewriters to get wrecked."

The fear of the unknown plagued them.

She could feel the anger welling up in her again. Her hands became hot and sparks flew from them.

The group looked petrified. The twins slowly nudged themselves backwards.

They're not only scared of me, but of my magic. They are scared of what they don't understand, she thought as Alex continued to talk.

She held up her hand, and he went silent. The feeling of being in control felt good. They wanted her to leave all this behind? There was no way. She wasn't about to go back to her husband, the money hungry, angry person he was. She finally had some power, and she was able to be in control and take charge. And that feeling was far too good to give up.

She let a smile creep over her face.

"I hear you all," she started gently. "But you need to know… I'm not going anywhere." She thrust her hand up into the air, and the sparks went flying up and burst like fireworks that gently floated down around them. They were scared, but she knew she had them.

"You can try to oppose me, but I don't recommend it."

"What are you going to do?" Alex said, taking a step towards her.

She glanced at Alex and winked. He let his shoulders relax and then she quickly put her hand out. Fire shot out of her hand and flew over to the eagle. He tried to duck out of the way, but there was no time. The fireball hit him hard and shot him back against the stone wall behind him. A circle of smouldering flesh and feathers appeared on his chest. He coughed and great plumes of smoke came out of him. Everyone around him panicked.

"It burns," he shrieked, trying to put it out by beating his wings on his chest. Everyone suddenly burst into action. James ran and grabbed some water, Cynthia grabbed a blanket and tried to put it out. Terrance looked at Sarith. Pleasure seeped out of her as she watched the sight.

"What have you done?" Terrance asked, while everyone else huddled around the eagle.

"Nothing. Yet."

Sarith headed out the door. She met Barabus's eyes, who stood against the back wall. No one tried to stop her and even if they had, she knew they couldn't.

Thirty-Four

"What do we do now?" Terrance asked, his voice shaking with fear.

"I don't know. We need to get him to the doctor."

Terrance pulled James aside so they could talk without everyone hearing them.

"The forest is super thick right now and the trip might be too hard on him. I don't think we can get all the way back to town. I don't know if he has enough time."

"What other choice do we have? If it had been any other animal, Alex could have flown him out. That would have been the fastest."

"But that's not an option now," Terrance said, his eyes darting back over to Alex. Smoke continued to spill out of him onto the floor and he was disappearing in a cloud.

"I have an idea," a voice said. Sam, a gopher, who was a fairly new dream-writer stood beside James.

"Sam, we're really busy. We don't have time…"

"Tunnels."

They both stopped, eyes snapping to him.

"I have a tunnel that goes from here to town. I didn't want to have to walk in the bad weather or have to go all around the rough terrain, so I made it on the weekend after I started here. It's not going to be big enough for you Terrance, but it's fine for me, James, and Alex. And it's a pretty direct route."

"Really?" Terrance asked.

"Yes. And we can dig more. It wouldn't take us long to do."

James and Terrance locked eyes.

"Underground tunnels. Could you dig out larger spaces, like rooms? Rooms big enough, for say, a whole bunch of typewriters to be set up in?" James asked.

Sam smiled wide. "Absolutely."

Terrance turned back to the group.

"Sam and James are going to take Alex to town. Cynthia, you follow them and when you get to town, I want you to round up every animal that digs and bring them back here through the tunnel. We have some digging to do."

James and Sam left, each of them carrying one side of Alex as he coughed and sputtered, sending clouds of smoke from him.

Even though the tunnels weren't large, they fit through it without a problem. James was amazed at how well made it was, and noticed how every so often, a support beam was put in place to support the roof.

"And you could make these bigger if you needed to?" James said, a bit winded.

"You betcha," Sam said, leading the way. They went up an incline, and he knocked on a spot on the wall. A door lifted and sunshine poured in. They walked up and out into the fresh air, heading towards town. The few that had stayed in town spotted them and came running. They helped get Alex towards the town's clinic.

"I'll stay with him," Woodrow said from behind him.

"I should get back. Now with Alex out of commission, I guess I'll be the one in charge," James said.

"I guess so," said Woodrow.

"Time to face the music."

Thirty-Five

Sarith ran. She didn't know where she was going, but she knew she couldn't stay. Tree branches slapped her face and her feet slipped on the exposed roots of the trees in the forest, but she couldn't stop. She couldn't think. In her mind, all she saw were flashes. Alex hit the wall on the far side of the room, and then the smoke came out of his mouth. It was beautiful for a moment, just a flash of a moment, until she saw what she had done. He screamed out in pain and more and more smoke came rushing out of him. He coughed, trying to get it out, but it just kept coming. Someone screamed. Another rushed over to him with a glass of water, but there wasn't enough water in the world to extinguish what she had done, and she knew that. Her magic was stronger than theirs.

She didn't know where she was headed until she burst from the forest and before her was the lake. The water was calm today. They wanted her to go home. They wanted her to leave. She might have made a mistake, but that didn't mean she should have to go. Sarith took a few deep breaths, trying to calm herself down, but it was no use. She let out a scream and watched as it sent vibrations across the water. The surrounding grass flattened, but then slowly came back up.

She could give in and let them have their peaceful place here, but what would that mean for her? She would go back to her world where everything was falling apart and she would once again be just simple Sarith, the woman whose voice didn't mean a thing and where she was powerless. Sarith hated that idea more than she could say. She would rather be anywhere else than there. And even though she was getting some resistance here, it was still better than being at home.

Then, an image came to mind. Her daughter's face. Her jet black hair that Melissa got from her and those dark eyes that were both beautiful and haunting. They were so much like Luke's, it was spooky. She knew she should go back, even if it was just for Melissa, but the thought of losing all this power was almost too much to handle.

She let herself fall to the ground and held her head in her hands.

A twig snapped behind her and she instantly stood, hands out, ready to fight.

"It's me," she heard as the figure came out of the shadows of the forest. Barabus stopped and met her eye.

"What?" she asked. "What could you possibly want? Or are you here just to make sure I go back home?"

"The way they have been treating you isn't right," Barabus said, coming and sitting beside her. "And they should recognize power when they see it. I do. I want to join forces with you."

"You want to join me?" she asked. She had seen his power before. She knew what he was capable of. "And what exactly do you see us doing together?"

"Well, after seeing you hurt Alex, I can tell something has changed. You are stronger and I think it's you getting your hands on that typewriter. We all know they are pretty magical to begin with, but this is different. Until tonight, you have never hurt anything, but now…"

"That wasn't exactly planned."

"No, but I can tell you enjoyed it," he said, shifting to face her better. "Your time is now. You need to take this new power and you need to take over. It's time."

Sarith had to admit, even if only to herself, the idea of that much power was enticing.

"And where would we even begin?" Sarith asked.

"We need to take over the dream-writing room and have you in charge. I'm going to do everything in my power to ensure it happens. We can start in the morning. We both need our rest."

"If you don't recall, my home is a pile of rubble."

"Well, I bet you could fix it now, but if you wanted something a bit… more your style, I know the perfect place."

Sarith followed the Barabus into the woods, but even in this low light she knew where he was taking her back to the castle.

Thirty-Six

Sarith and Barabus arrived at the castle a short time later, but in those moments, she saw he was right. She was stronger than she had been even the day before. Something about writing the dream had given her more power.

The silence around the castle was unsettling.

"Why would you bring me back here after everything that just happened?" Sarith asked, unsure if she even wanted to step foot into the place.

"Just wait. You'll see."

They walked around the side of the building to a secondary entrance, tucked amongst ivy and overgrown weeks. Sarith hadn't seen this part of the castle before. The place had candles lit along the walls, but even the smallest sound from her shoes seemed to echo across the walls and down the hall.

"Here," he said, stopping in front of a door. He pushed it open and inside was a large four corner bed with draping curtains and a fireplace in the corner. The room was chilly, so with a flick of her wrist, she lit the logs placed in it. "I don't know if it's up to your liking, but we can work on it. I knew you needed somewhere to stay quick, so I just threw it together."

"You made this for me?" she said, looking into his deep brown eyes.

"Like I said, it's not much…" His voice trailed off.

"It's fantastic." She grinned widely at him and clasped her hands in front of her.

"After you left, I came to this area and put it together. I was thinking, with your magical force, and my persuasion, we'll get most of the dream-writers on our side. We'll make them join our side."

"I think you might be right."

"And we can do it in such a way they won't know what hit them," he said.

He was right. Together, there was so much more they could do. She loved his initiative, too. He was planning in ways she didn't expect or had even thought of yet. Tonight had been too much of a whirlwind for her to even start thinking about all this. Partnering up with him would be perfect, though. If he could think this fast on his feet and come up with plans and execute them, she could be the power to his brains.

"I think you're onto something here. After a good night's rest, we could really do something."

"I agree. I'm just the next room over, but in the morning we can do what's needed."

Sarith waited until he left before crawling into bed. This definitely wasn't what she had planned, but he was right. She had the power. No one had even gotten close to her ability and if they were going to stop her, they would have. There was no going back. It was now or never and never was not a choice.

* * *

The next morning, Sarith awoke as the sun shone through an opening in the curtains. She rolled over and for a moment, it felt like she was in her room at home and that everything she had experienced was just a dream.

Only as she sat up and stretched did she see she wasn't at home. The reality of the last few days came crashing like the ceiling of her home had.

Sarith quickly got out of bed and rinsed her face in the basin Barabus must have brought in at some point. She fixed her hair and smoothed her clothes. She would have to make some new ones at some point. The ones in her home were probably destroyed. Today she would go back in the light of day and see if anything could be salvaged.

A knock at her door brought her out of her thoughts. Barabus poked his head in.

"I'm sorry to intrude, but you need to see this," Barabus said, motioning for her to accompany him.

She followed, leaving her thoughts behind for now.

Thirty-Seven

He guided them back to the section of the castle they'd visited the night before. He hesitated, then stepped closer, gently pushing open the door.

Goosebumps washed like waves over her as she pushed past him. This time, it was empty. Every table, every typewriter, every enchanted box. All of it was gone. The only thing that remained were a few dust bunnies in the corners.

Barabus spun and walked down the hall. He pushed open door after door. Each room that once had been full of typewriters and dream-writers was now empty.

"They took everything!" Sarith said, following behind him.

Barabus's eyes were wild with anger. He ran ahead of her. Sarith didn't even have to ask to know where he was going. She ran behind him and finally caught up, reaching out for the door first.

The mailroom was still there, still intact. They both walked in and checked the tubes. They were still hooked up and working. The enchanted boxes sat nearby.

Sarith couldn't believe it. They needed these or they couldn't get the information on what to write for the dreams. Why would they leave something like this behind?

The sound of footsteps met her ears at the same time as Barabus. They stood, ready for a fight.

James appeared in the doorway, clearly not expecting to see anyone there. He jumped back and went to run. Barabus darted and grabbed him, spinning him.

"What did you do with it all?" Barabus snarled down at James.

Sarith expected James to be fearful, but somehow she was nothing but calm.

"Wouldn't you like to know?" James said.

"Let him go," Sarith said, waltzing over. "You can tell us willingly or I can force you. Your choice."

Barabus let him go with a shove and James stumbled back. He recovered quickly and straightened his fur.

"You will never find us," James said.

"Maybe so, but you will not get the last say in this." Sarith turned towards the tubes. She looked back at James. "Won't you need this tube system to know what to write?"

"You can't stop us from using it."

"Ha! That's what you think," she said, standing beside him, both now looking at the maze of tubes. Sarith raised her hands and slowly a glowing wall appeared between them and the tubes.

"What are you doing?" James asked, carefully approaching it.

"What do you think I'm doing? I'm taking over," Sarith said, grinning.

James put his hand on the glowing surface and was shot backwards, past Sarith, and to the wall behind them.

Sarith knew she had power, but she wasn't expecting that. Although, seeing it was pretty amazing. It was definitely stronger than last night. She could do almost anything she wanted now, and no one could take that away from her.

"This is mine. This entire castle. It's not my fault you didn't get everything out of here yet. Whatever's left, count it as mine."

James stumbled to his feet and slowly backed towards the door.

"Tell everyone this is it. From now on, you answer to me."

James took off. Barabus made to move, but Sarith shook her head no. Once he was out of sight, she looked at him.

"We need James to tell them all what is now reality here. This is my world now, and they are going to answer to me."

Barabus smiled and walked over to her. "And I'll do anything I can to help you," he said.

Thirty-Eight

Sarith scanned her army. The courtyard was full of troops training. The sounds of them grunting and exerting themselves filled the air. She loved that sound over the last few months. After taking over the castle, Barabus had helped her make it her own. He was the one who had believed in her the most. No one in her life ever had.

Since that night, the mailroom remained heavily guarded by her army. She had to be sure none of the animals could get back in and destroy what she had built. Having it had given her leverage, she needed to make them write the dreams she wanted. All she wanted at this point was that same surge of power she had felt the night she had written the nightmare.

So, she took the information from the mailroom and wrote it into a dream with a nightmarish twist and sent it off.

If they did as required, the beast would come back bigger than he had been the day before, and she could feel and see her magic getting stronger. Making them send the dreams back in the enchanted boxes ensured they wrote them, too. She would read the dreams and see the fear in the words and she would smile. Sarith loved it. It was the only thing that would give her the surge of power again. It was the only thing that would make her feel alive. And she loved it more than anything else.

As she watched the army training for battle, she felt the surge of power again. An entire team of writers would be working right now. Smiling, she looked over at Barabus. He nodded back to her. For the first time in a very long time, she finally felt at peace. She reached to the chain around her neck and pulled it out. The ruby stone in the necklace caught in the light. Maybe Miles had made the right decision about not selling the store to her after all.

Acknowledgements

Writing a villain origin story can be a bit scary. It's not your typical tale were there is a happy ending and everyone has a feel-good moment at the end, but after writing my first book, I just knew Sarith would want her story told. We all have things happen in our lives that can feel overwhelming but it's how we react to those moments that shape where we end up, and what our story is.

I dedicate this book to my dad who I lost in the fall of 2023. He may not have read my words, but my dad got to see my first book in print. Through the years, he always believed in me and my dream of writing a novel. I'm glad he got to see that happen. James's journey through grief, while not exactly like mine, had some similarities. Grief can drown you in a tidal wave if you let it, but I'm thankful I could use those hard moments to write the words I needed for his story and to work through some of those feelings.

Thank you to everyone who helped me with this novel. Your encouragement, love, and support helped me so much along the way.

I especially want to thank Hazel Vale for her help editing. I've *started to realize that* I need your *eyes* to *look* through the words of my novel because the amount of repetitive words I use can be *terrifying*

Author Bio

Kelly Dowswell is a writer from southwestern Ontario, with a background in pagination (page layout) for her city's two local newspapers. When she isn't drinking tea and spending time with her husband and two sons, she's writing short stories and novels. She has also had two short stories published in the anthology Masquerade that she helped compile, and her debut novel Written in Ink was published in 2023.